FLICKER

Other books by Len Boswell

A Grave Misunderstanding
Skeleton
The Leadership Secrets of Squirrels

FLICKER

A Paranormal Mystery

Len Boswell

© 2014, 2017 by Len Boswell. All rights reserved.

Originally published as an ebook under the pen name L. Rett Boswell

This is a work of fiction. Names, characters, businesses, places, events and incidents are either the products of the author's imagination or used in a fictitious manner. Any resemblance to actual persons, living or dead, or actual events is purely coincidental.

To all I love without condition
To all I love without omission

Never doubt

"Then away out in the woods I heard that kind of sound that a ghost makes when it wants to tell about something that's on its mind and can't make itself understood, and so can't rest easy in its grave, and has to go about that way every night grieving."
—Mark Twain, *The Adventures of Huckleberry Finn*

"The murdered do haunt their murderers, I believe. I know that ghosts have wandered on earth."
—Emily Bronte, *Wuthering Heights*

"Perhaps they all come back on moonlit nights."
—Lucy Maud Montgomery, *Anne of Avonlea*

"Everything that happens once can never happen again. But everything that happens *twice* will surely happen a third time."
—Paulo Coelho, *The Alchemist*

PROLOGUE

When she entered the diner, every head instinctively turned to look at her, not so much for her dazzling beauty, which was evident right from the start, but for the simple fact that she was still behind the wheel of a pink Cadillac convertible with nothing but momentum on its mind.

The diner's thin metallic skin had offered little resistance, peeling back with preternatural ease, as if the hole it was creating had been preordained, each atom aligning and clicking into place just so to create a hole that in the weeks that followed would be called the "caddy hole," a hole remarkable for the fact that its outline could only have been made by a Cadillac.

The car had made its way down the aisle between the booths on the left and the counter on the right, people leaping for safety, its left fender demolishing booth after booth, splintered pine, Formica shards, and red leather flying, while the right fender lifted stool after stool, sending them into the air, red seats spinning, creating a brief illusion of stool-powered flight before they crashed down on the counter, shattering the pie case, fruit shrapnel and meringue flying everywhere, coating walls, ceiling, and the customers retreating to the far end of the diner.

Through all this, she kept her eyes fixed on her target.

CHAPTER 1

THE FIRE CRACKLED, BLAZED, SENDING SPARKS and briefly glowing cinders upward through the trees in a column of gray smoke that blew gently eastward as it rose from the canopy. No matter how close he stood to the fire, he could not seem to extract any warmth from it, even in this summer heat. And now they had arrived, the two of them, that widow woman and some younger man, no doubt a potential buyer, someone he'd have to deal with sooner or later, though he was thinking sooner. The woman was easy to identify, even from this distance, her pink Caddy a dead giveaway. He thought about that—*dead giveaway*—and snorted. *Bitch*.

The man was also easy to identify as a potential buyer. You could tell he was trying not to get too excited, but any man who spent his time looking almost exclusively at that old diner while almost completely ignoring the beautiful woman standing next to him, well, you may as well tattoo "buyer" on his forehead. *Or damn fool*, he thought.

And the both of them made him angry, angrier than he had been in weeks, months, years. He could barely resist the impulse to burst from the tree line where he stood, out of sight, poking at the fire with his gnarled old walking stick, and deal with them both, just like that and be done with it. He had waited too many years—too many *god damned* years—to end this once and for all. Still, there were rules to be followed. *Fools rush in, right?* Well, he was not about to do that. He'd have his revenge, though, no question. *And fuck those fearful angels, wherever they may tread.* He raised his stick and pointed it at them, the stick bouncing in the air twice as if from a shotgun's kick. "Pow, pow!" he whispered, curling his lips in a way that no one would interpret as friendly.

When Charlie Brace first saw his dream, his diner, it was up on blocks in a sunbaked vacant lot behind a gas station, surrounded by 50-gallon drums of spent oil, looking to him so dilapidated and fragile that a single nudge would reduce it to scrap. But this is what you got for $30,000 these days, and Charlie Brace had just that and enough left over from his inheritance to transport her to the site and fix her up.

Her.

He didn't know why he used *her* when he talked about diners. If pushed, he would probably say there was something graceful about them, a deep curviness, an abiding gentleness, an almost motherly warmth. But clearly, with this diner, on this day, that would have been the dream talking, a love-is-blind delusion.

The widow of the previous owner could see this in his eyes, the look of the dreamer, so she knew there would be no haggling, despite the fact that she was prepared to accept half the asking price just to get this diner out of her life.

She had been a beauty once. Charlie had seen that right away. Tall and shapely, with penetrating blue eyes and close-cropped, neatly coiffed brown hair, she retained an incandescent sexuality that no doubt had caused many a fistfight in her youth. And despite the age difference—she must be, what, fifteen years older—he could see himself easily caught in her spell, just as surely as he was caught now in the spell of the diner.

"Bill loved this diner," she said. "I don't know why."

"Yes," Charlie said absently, his eyes fixed on the diner. "Don't you worry; I'll take good care of her."

She glanced over at him. He reminded her of Bill in many ways, but certainly not physically. Where Bill had been short and muscular, this man, this Mr. Brace, was tall and thin, as hollow-cheeked as a long-distance runner, but with a quick, engaging smile quite unlike Bill's, which was more of a smirk and came so rarely, especially in those last months. Looking at him now—the way he moved his hands, those long, graceful fingers, the boyish gleam in his pale eyes, his lips—*oh, his lips!*—she felt something stir in her, a heat long dormant. What would it be like to share this dream with him, to hold him close? She shook off that thought. He was so young. Still.

"Yes, I bet you will," she said. He made no reply; just stood there staring at the diner, that little smile on his face.

She cleared her throat. "So . . ."

"Oh," Charlie said, realizing she was ready to talk money. "$30,000 is it?"

She didn't want to meet his eye. Eyes reveal everything, the very soul of a person, and she didn't want him to see the desperation in hers. So she looked at the diner instead. "Yes," she said, as firmly and matter-of-factly as she could. "Yes, that's the price."

"Then we have a deal," he said with an ever-broadening smile, *yes! yes! yes!* screaming in his head.

A little laugh burst from her then, which she quickly covered up with her hand. Charlie didn't notice. He was already closing the distance between himself and the diner, to lay hands on her, to claim her as his.

The widow called after him. "The papers will be ready in a couple of days. My lawyer will call you."

"Yes, ma'am," he said, looking back at her. "The sooner, the better."

Had he continued looking at her, which he didn't, he would have seen her expression suddenly change, becoming almost somber.

"Mr. Brace, promise me one thing."

"Anything, ma'am," he said, still looking away, running his hand along the side of the diner, which seemed unusually cold for an August afternoon.

"Promise me you'll be careful."

"Sure, sure," he said, completely distracted by the diner—it was *his* now. Then, realizing what had been said, he turned back to her again. "Ma'am?"

But there would be no answer, no clarification. She had already turned on her heels and was striding briskly for her car, a vintage pink Caddy, a throwback to the glory days of diners, long gone now, leaving him standing there, a man and his diner in the fading light of day.

As she climbed into her car and started the engine, Charlie shrugged, thinking *that's weird*, but then shouted, "I will."

She nodded, forcing a little smile, and drove away, the sound of the engine gradually giving way to cicada song, the final throes of courtship in the trees, leaving him alone with the diner—*his* diner.

Or so he thought.

"They say the moon will be full tonight," a voice behind him said.

Startled, Charlie spun around, reflexively clenching his fists but quickly realizing that the man standing beside the diner was hardly a threat, even with the tall walking stick he held loosely at his side, which was nothing more than a tree limb roughly whittled at both ends.

"I mean, if you plan to stay out here that long, you'll have fine light for it. Nothin' like a diner in moonlight, to my mind. And come a full moon, this one here will glow, soft like, like it was alive."

He was old and frail, homeless probably, a trash-picker certainly, the burlap sack he held in one hand clear evidence of that. His clothing was tattered, his trousers held up by a length of black electrical wire, the exposed copper ends twisted and glinting in the fading sunlight. Despite the heat he wore what looked like the remains of a red checkered table cloth across his shoulders. He had a pointed gray beard, thick and full at the cheek but scraggily and seemingly disappearing at the ends, halfway down his chest, as if the hair had said, "Enough, this is where I draw the line." A red skullcap pulled down over his ears gave him a gnome-like appearance. He smelled of wood fire and sweat.

Charlie didn't know what to make of him, or what to do next. "Um, actually, I was about to leave."

The man pursed his lips and shrugged. "Makes no never mind to me," he said. "I'll keep an eye on her for you. Camp's not far from here." He pointed vaguely toward the woods, where Charlie could see smoke rising from the trees, and above them a murder of crows wheeling in a wide circle through the smoke.

"By the fire, you mean?"

The man looked puzzled, and turned to look at the smoke. "Naw, that's not mine. Some other feller, and I'd recommend you steer clear of him and his friends. Not your friendly types, if you know what I mean. Not all of us on the road are *gentle* souls." He seemed to find humor in that, offering Charlie a chuckle and a wink.

Charlie didn't laugh or return the wink, not wanting to extend the conversation further. "Well, then, I guess I'll leave her to you and be on my way," Charlie said, turning toward his car and walking away. "Have a nice evening."

The man took off his hat and scratched his head vigorously, as if to rid himself of vermin, then pulled it back on. "So you bought her, is that it?"

Charlie turned, and squinted at him. "You were listening?"

"Not at all, saw the two of you from my camp, is all."

"And you figured that out from way over there?" Charlie said, incredulous.

"Ha! I'm right, ain't I?" he clucked.

"Yes, but—"

"I just *know* things sometimes," he said, tapping a finger on the side of his nose. "Like that woman you were with. Seen her dozens of times, right here with that sweet Caddy of hers. Pussy Pink is what I call it."

Charlie blinked. He never used the word.

"But always—*always*—alone and so sad," he continued. "Seen her cry here more than once, her hand touching the diner kind of reverent like, like it was a gravestone. Downright touching it was."

"So you live here, in the woods?"

The man glanced back at the trees. "Not hardly, no, but I stop here on my travels, mostly to see the diner again. Reminds me of the good times—and some bad, too—when I was young, or at least younger, and still had sap enough to court the ladies. And I'd be lying if I said the woman had nothin' to do with my stopping here time and again. She's quite the looker, don't you think?"

Charlie had to agree. "Yes, she's a handsome woman."

"Handsome?" the man snorted. "Hell, boy, *handsome* is for women who've lost their juice, and a damn river still flows in that one. I seen the way she looked at you, and you at her—don't deny it—so don't be giving me that handsome crap."

Charlie shook his head. "And you saw *all* of that from the woods?"

"As clear as if I'd been standin' right next to you."

"I was just buying this diner."

The man chuckled and threw up his hands. "Whatever you say, young man." He turned, started to walk away, and then stopped, looking back at Charlie. "One thing . . ."

"Yes?"

"What are your plans for her?"

"None," Charlie said. "Like I said, I just bought the diner from her."

The man shook his head. "No, no, I meant *her*," he said, pointing at the diner. "What are your plans for her?"

Charlie tried to recover, but knew his face was flushing. "Oh, I plan to move her and fix her up."

The man looked concerned. "Move her? Where to exactly?"

"Not far, really, to Maryland, a place on Route 1, north of Laurel."

"Well, if that don't beat all. Why there?"

Charlie did not want to get into the details of his inheritance with this man, which would only lead to more and more questions about him, his grandfather, and who knew what else. "Own some land there."

The man nodded. "Can't argue with that, but *not far* is still quite a hike for a man on foot. Still, I may see you down the road sometime. I'd love to see how you fix her up." He glanced over at the diner, a sad look on his face, then back at Charlie, extending his hand. "Well, then . . ."

Charlie shook his hand, surprised by the firmness of the man's grip and how cold it was.

CHAPTER 2

THE WIDOW'S LAWYER, A YOUNG GO-GETTER with slicked-back black hair and a neatly groomed goatee, appropriately named Johnny Shark, Esq., pushed paper after paper across the desk for Charlie to sign, his diamond-studded cuff links sparkling in the sunlight that slanted through the windows.

He was taller than Charlie by nearly a foot, enough to place him at the elite height of professional basketball players, but the hunch of his shoulders suggested a more sedentary, scholarly life style.

From the appearance of his office—every surface nearly bare of papers, a lone diploma hanging behind his desk the only decoration—he seemed to be just starting out. That, and his obvious youth.

"Note in this one that she's lowered the price to $28,000," he said. "Compensation for the signs."

"The signs?"

"Yes, the neon signs are apparently busted.

"All of them?"

"Yeah, all three apparently went on the fritz at the same time. A lot of buzzing and flickering, she said. Never got around to fixing them. Says you should probably discard them or at least get a good electrician or neon guy to take a look at 'em."

"All right, that's very nice of her."

The lawyer picked up another paper and pushed it across the desk. "Okay, sign here, initial there," he said, then pushed another paper at him, and another, and another, the monotony of it interrupted only by his near incessant throat-clearings, the product, Charlie surmised, of heavy smoking.

Charlie dutifully signed, initialed, and pushed each paper back until there were no more to sign.

"That's it, then, Mr. Brace," Shark said, clearing his throat again and then reaching across the desk to first shake Charlie's hand and then hand him neatly collated and paper-clipped copies of the documents.

Charlie took them and stood up. "Thanks," he said.

"Right," Shark said. "If you ever have any questions—or need a lawyer—just let me know."

"No problem." Charlie turned and started for the door.

"Oh, wait a minute," Shark said, grabbing a folder from his desk drawer and holding it out toward Charlie. "Grace, that is to say Mrs. Sharp, wants you to have this, says it's very important that you review everything in here carefully. In fact, she said read it *very* carefully."

"Why's that?

Shark shrugged. "Dunno."

Charlie took the folder and read the yellow sticky note attached to it: *Mr. Brace, thought you should have this info, just in case. It's important! Call if you have any questions, 410-874-1632. Best of luck, Grace Sharp.*

"Humph, a 410 number. Didn't know she lived in Maryland."

"Yeah, she just moved there, not far from your property in fact."

"That's great. I can invite her to the diner opening, then."

Shark looked at him strangely, forcing a smile. "Well, sure, I guess you could do that. Yeah, why not?"

"Okay, then," Charlie said, tucking the folder under his arm. "Thanks for all your help on this."

"No problem, Mr. Brace, and best of *luck* with that diner." There was something odd about the way he said it, as if he was suggesting that Charlie would need more than luck.

Among the papers in the folder was documentation on the history of the diner, which had been purchased and sold three times since its manufacture by the Bramson Engineering Company of Oyster Bay, New York. A faded company brochure hawked the features of a diner "built like a battleship."

Bramson Diners Have It
- Designed to produce profits
- Custom built at mass production prices
- Laid out by experts
- Cheerful atmosphere interiors
- Planned seating

Exterior Construction
- Stainless steel built
- Aluminum heat deflection roof
- Aluminized aluminum doors, Kawneer made
- Slanted thermopane windows, 1 inch thick
- Large vestibule, 2 door entrance
- Lighting around entire diner and vestibule

Interior Construction
- Formica with stainless steel trim
- Fiberglass insulation throughout
- Sanitary Terrazo floors throughout
- Indirect fluorescent lighting throughout
- Animastats for air conditioning

Dimensions
51 ft. X 17 ft. approx., overall
Capacity
60 customers

Included in the brochure was an artist's rendition of a completed diner, which looked like an overly large shoebox with rounded corners, a stainless steel skin, and large windows spanning the front and sides. A stainless steel cube with two doors—the vestibule—was attached front and center, looking like an afterthought the size of two phone booths.

The diner had sprung to life as the Last Stop Diner, custom-built for a Thomas Davis of South Windham, Connecticut. Judging from the documents, the diner had been mostly standard, but

Davis had requested that the large windows along the right side be replaced by a solid, though thin, stainless steel wall, to block "an unsightly view," of what the documents didn't say. A news photo showing Davis and his white-aproned staff outside his gleaming new diner showed a low stone wall to the right of the diner, looking more sightly than unsightly.

No one in the photograph was smiling, their pensive faces staring out at Charlie.

Just one year later Davis had died and ownership had been transferred to a Becky Swanson, who moved the diner to Flemington, New Jersey, renaming it "Becky's." The one photo in the folder showed a heavy and glum looking Becky serving a piece of pie to a barefoot little girl in overalls. Apparently, Becky had good reason to be glum. The diner failed after just eighteen months and was sold at an amazingly low price to a Chester McAllister, who inexplicably put it up on blocks and let it sit in the corner of a warehouse for years before selling it to Bill Sharp for a still cheaper price.

Sharp moved the old diner to Phillipsburg, Pennsylvania, replacing the round neon "Becky's" sign with a rectangular sign that ran the length of the diner proclaiming "Sharp's Diner" in red neon, flanked on one side by "Open 24 Hours" and the other by "Good Eats," both in green neon. In the lone photograph of Sharp's Diner, the first "S" in "Sharp's Diner" was burned out, as was the first "o" in "Good Eats." The "Open 24 Hours" sign was not visible.

Sharp's Diner apparently flourished in its first year, the diner being the new new-thing in Phillipsburg. News clippings from the local paper, *The Philippic*, hailed its coming, its food, and its congenial owners. One clipping showed Bill Sharp and a younger Grace Sharp smiling into the camera, Bill proudly holding up a Sharpsburger while Grace poured a cup of coffee for a customer.

Another clipping, dated eight months later, showed a smiling Bill Sharp holding up a plaque proclaiming "Best Coffee," a secret blend, the story said, "ground fresh each day to the delight of patrons, one and all."

I'll have to ask her about that, Charlie thought.

Other clippings showed a little league baseball team sponsored by the diner, a photo of Bill sitting in a booth with the governor, who was there to glad-hand the customers for votes, and a photo of a line of men, women, and children, all looking down and out, each holding a plate ready to receive the food being dished up and plopped down by Bill and Grace. The caption read, "Diner owners serve up Thanksgiving for the less fortunate."

The last clipping, dated twenty-two months from the diner's opening, reported the untimely death of Bill Sharp.

DINER OWNER COLLAPSES, DIES
William Wade Sharp, 40, owner-proprietor of Sharp's Diner on Route 3, collapsed and died of an apparent heart attack Saturday evening while working in his diner. Willie

Morton, a short-order cook, tried to revive him but was unsuccessful. Sharp's wife, Grace, was unavailable for comment. Funeral arrangements are pending.

Charlie wondered why she'd included this clipping. It seemed odd to him that she wouldn't want to have it for herself, and it didn't tell him anything he didn't know already.

He looked at the date again. His diner had apparently been sitting on blocks for five years. He'd have to take a closer look at the roof and the window caulking.

CHAPTER 3

WHEN CHARLIE RETURNED TO THE SITE at daybreak a few weeks later to watch the transport company load the diner into the bed of the biggest truck he'd ever seen, there was no sign of the old man. Smoke was still rising through the trees, though, and he thought he could see more than one person moving near the fire. He thought briefly of trudging over there, but then thought better of it, remembering the old man's warning.

The loading process took nearly two hours, but then they were on the road, with Charlie in a lead pickup truck equipped with flashing lights and a big sign that read "Wide Load," warning traffic to stay clear.

The trip to Laurel was painfully slow, and boring. The driver of the pickup was not one for conversation, even about the weather. But when Charlie saw a line of smoke climbing into the sky, the fourth or fifth he'd seen on the trip, he had to ask, "So, does this state allow open burning? There seem to be fires going all along here."

The driver had grunted, glanced at the smoke, and said, "dunno." End of conversation.

Fortunately, by late afternoon, they were pulling onto Charlie's land. An hour later, the diner sat neatly on a concrete pad Charlie had had installed, looking like it had been there forever.

After the workers left, Charlie walked around the diner, looking at it from every angle, gauging what needed to be done next. There was the matter of the parking lot, and some trees that would need to be cleared, not to mention signage, utility hookups, and a whole host of repairs, large and small, inside and out.

As the light faded and the moon peeked over the trees, he heard a sharp, wood-on-wood sound coming from the woods, where a thin column of smoke was rising deep within.

He'd have to look into that, *but not tonight*, he thought. *I'm bushed*.

They all watched Charlie as he walked around the diner, and then one of them said, "so when're we gonna do it?"

The answer came swiftly, the gnarled walking stick slammed against a nearby tree. "I told you, I *have* a plan."

"Just askin', is all."

"Yeah, we've been waitin' so long," said another.

"Shit, you always have a plan," mumbled yet another one under her breath."

"What's that?" the old man snarled.

Silence.

He looked from one face to another, to every god damned one of them, and saw the same look on every face. Despite their number, they seemed to behave like one organism, an organism he would just as soon crush under his heel than listen to its whining and that look of—*what?*

Hunger. A deep, abiding hunger.

He shook his stick at them. "I know what you *want*, you miserable sons of bitches, and the time will come for that. You'll have your *fill* of it if I know that bitch. But now—*now*—we can't, *won't* rush this. We gotta get it right this time, down to the last detail, understand? So we take it slow, follow the plan."

"But what *is* the plan?" said someone way in the back.

He sighed heavily. *Here we go again*, he thought, *here we go again*. But he knew it was time.

"Okay, okay," he said. "You know the drill, mostly. You'll all have a job, same as last time."

"*Last time* it didn't work," said a young woman leaning against a tree.

The old man squinted at her. *Little bitch*. "Last time we didn't get it right, this time we will, you just wait and see."

He looked away from her, addressing the others. "Now, who wants to volunteer for an inside job?"

CHAPTER 4

MOST BUSINESSES, IF THEIR INTENT IS SUCCESS, go through an elaborate process, call it a test drive through the demographics, to find a site that, for them, screams the mantra for success: *location, location, location*.

Charlie, on the other hand, just plopped his diner down on the one piece of land he owned, a heavily treed acre at a "T" intersection on Route 1 handed down to him by his grandfather, who had purchased it long ago, when bear and deer and elk still roamed the woods. His grandfather had always wanted to build a getaway cabin there, but a man with mouths to feed and callused hands must give way to the here and now and the steady creep of the future.

By the 1950s, the property was little more than an oasis of green in a heavily commercialized jumble of car dealerships, auto repair garages, bowling alleys, skating rinks, gas stations, and a host of billboards promoting Marlboro's, Coppertone, and Chevrolets to pale smokers who wanted to but never did see the U.S.A in their Chevrolets, preferring to spend their days in the shade and their nights huddled around the television, filling ashtray after ashtray with little pieces of their lives, as Milton Berle mugged in drag.

Only the billboards had changed since then, it seemed, the Marlboro Man riding off into a cancerous sunset, replaced now by a happy couple who had just purchased a new home in Vesper

Downs, their lives now controlled by a balloon loan that would keep them up nights.

Even now, though, the area lacked an all-night eatery, a place where shift workers, college kids, truckers, late-night bowlers, and insomniacs could find a warm place, a hot cup of coffee, and food that would stick to their ribs, calories be damned.

Charlie positioned the diner so that the lights of oncoming cars approaching from the south, along the vertical of the "T," would not blind or annoy his customers. He had Thomas Davis's custom wall to thank for that. He built a U-shaped parking lot around the diner, to set it off from the trees and give everyone approaching from the west or east along the horizontal of the "T" time enough to see the sign and hit the brakes.

Charlie loved trees, so he cut down only the bare minimum. The decision, or more correctly the *act*—because Charlie did not give the matter much thought—left him with a parking lot that would accommodate just thirty cars, half the seating capacity of the diner. As a result, the diner never looked too empty, creating the impression that this diner *must* have great food. And on Saturdays, when the college crowd poured in after the game, and especially on Sundays, when the place would fill with churchgoers fresh from brimstone oratory, loosening their Sunday-best ties, and later their belts, the overflowing parking lot and the long line of cars along both shoulders created the impression that this really must be the place to eat, so next time, next time, the hungry should arrive a little earlier. *Advantage heathens.*

The downside, if there really was a downside, to the way he positioned the diner was that he now needed three neon signs, one facing east toward the bowling alley, one facing west toward Brown's Chevrolet, and one facing south and tilted back a bit so people coming down the hill from the college could see the sign clearly. That sign, in emerald green neon, said simply "Diner," while the other two shouted, in red neon, "Open 24 Hours" and the diner's new name, the "Red Oak Diner," a name Charlie had chosen to reflect the diner's décor—screaming red leatherette stools and booth benches—and the dominant species in the horseshoe of trees left standing.

Fortunately, the $2,000 discount Grace Sharp had given him was just enough to cover the manufacture and installation of the signs, which were up and glowing in no time, thanks to the quick work of the sign company, Neon Discounters, and its chief installer, Larry Waits.

Charlie couldn't afford a paved parking lot, so he filled it with gravel trucked in by a friend of a friend's cousin, a man of enormous girth, who wanted nothing more in return than a free blue-plate special on Saturday nights. Charlie was happy to oblige.

While the man dumped, graded, and leveled, Charlie busied himself with the interior, which was in remarkably good condition despite its time on the blocks.

The refrigerator, an old Belding Hall, still worked, as did the six-burner stove, two Wolf grills, and the deep fryer. The exhaust fan in the grill hood needed to be replaced, but otherwise the hood, a gleaming German-silver Monel, shone as brightly as it must have done the day it rolled off the assembly line. There were a few cigarette burns on the Formica counter, but all the stainless steel sinks and work tables were near pristine.

The counter stools and booth cushions were another matter entirely. The leatherette was cracked, the padding was shot, and each and every stool seat wobbled. The friend of a friend's cousin had a solution for that, though, bringing in his neighbor's son's girlfriend's father, an upholsterer, who re-covered the stools and booths in red Naugahyde, giving the diner a cloying new-car smell, and de-wobbled the stools for the cost of materials and another blue-plate special deal. Charlie would at least have two regular customers.

Two weeks later, after what seemed endless scrubbing and mopping, Charlie's diner gleamed inside and out. All he really needed now was a supply of food and enough cooks, waitresses, and kitchen help to fulfill the diner's 24-hour promise.

And customers, lots of customers.

CHAPTER 5

ADS IN THE LOCAL PAPER, *THE INQUISITOR*, and in the college paper, *The Cougar*, and especially the Now Hiring signs facing west, east, and south had brought a steady stream of diner wannabes seeking full-time and part-time employment.

Some Charlie rejected almost immediately.

Larry Thompson, a cook from Gaylord's Indian Palace, had a decent work history but farted twice during the brief interview. "Sorry," he had said. "Better out than in, right?" Charlie had nodded and sent him on his way, making a mental note about Gaylord's.

Susan Mollicker, a college pom-pom girl, had no signs of intelligent life between her poms. "Do I take orders *and* serve the customers?"

Pam Franz, a trucker's wife, was looking for a job to fill the dead space in her life, on her terms. "Of course, I can't work when Bill's home."

Other candidates seemed a perfect fit, or at least close.

There was **Jeanie Beene**, a middle-aged career waitress who had pushed into the diner with the swagger of a drill sergeant and the big-boned, barrel-chested body to back it up. Destroying this military image completely, however, and turning it near comical, was her hair, an explosion of gray streaked with the last vestiges of a youthful brown and styled in a fashion popular thirty years earlier, as if she had chosen, consciously or unconsciously, to freeze herself in time. Her eyebrows had been tweezed to near extinction in seemingly single-hair arcs above her eyes that gave her a forever startled look. She wore no lipstick, but had rouged each cheek in attempt to add color to her otherwise pale complexion. She said she worked at The Dixie Pig down the road, famous for its shredded and minced beef, pork, and chicken barbecue sandwiches, and was looking for a better-paying position.

"I've been a soup jockey for twenty-seven years, drawin' mud and dolin' Magoo since you were a little pup."

Charlie blinked. "What?"

"Mud, Magoo . . . Oh, I get it. Sorry, I thought you'd know the lingo. *Shit*."

Charlie guessed that mud was coffee, which pleased Jeanie no end, but Magoo stumped him.

"Magoo is custard pie, dear."

"I would never have guessed . . ."

"No matter, the lingo is between me and what you would call the cook. Say, have you hired an angel yet?"

"An angel?"

"A sandwich man, dear, a sandwich man. Look, three things make a diner hum: a good sandwich man, great pies, and most important, a terrific cup of coffee."

"Angel, Magoo, and Mud."

Jeanie laughed. "That's it, honey. Of course, when it comes to pies, the most important is Eve with a lid on, Eve with a moldy lid, and Eve with a hat on.

"And that would be?"

"Apple pie, apple pie with cheese, and apple pie with ice cream—all three have to be great or you're in big trouble—unless you've got the best damn coffee for miles around."

"Well, I think I have *great* coffee."

She gave him a skeptical look and asked for a cup, which he served to her in one of the coffee mugs he'd picked up at a restaurant supply company out in Clarksville the day before. No one, it seemed, wanted these mugs, which had an oak leaf theme, so he had picked them up, complete with matching bowls and plates, for a song. He bought the coffee there as well, another bargain, and it was not half bad.

Unfortunately, Jeanie Beene did not find it half good, screwing up her face and setting the mug down hard. "Don't tell me," she said, picking up the mug again and sniffing the coffee as if she were judging a fine wine. "Meyer's Black Label, from that supply house out on Route 108."

"Yes, how did you—"

"Because nothing in this world smells as awful or tastes as bad as Meyer's, is how."

"Humph, it tastes fine to me."

"D-T-D."

"Huh?"

"Dead Tongue Disease. Your taste buds have gone south if you think that's good coffee." She stood and began buttoning her coat. "I'm sorry, Mr. Brace, but the coffee is a deal breaker."

"What?"

"I can't work here with coffee like that." She started toward the door.

"Wait, I can change the coffee. And I'd really like you to join us here at The Red Oak."

"Well, when you get better coffee, give me a call." And with that, she walked briskly out of the diner with Charlie on her heels, crunched across the parking lot, and drove away without another word, despite Charlie's protests. Charlie stood there watching her drive away, then turned back to the diner, and noticed a column of smoke rising through the trees for the first time in days. *That old man?* Charlie thought. *The other guy?* He shook his head. No, they couldn't have gotten here that quickly. *Must be a local.* He made a mental note to check it out later, but for now, he had to get back to the interviews.

Other candidates were not so particular about their coffee, and he signed them up on the spot.

Chloe Munson, just out of high school, was the first waitress he hired. She was as tall and shapely as she was sweet and naïve, but with an earnestness that won Charlie over. That, and her ample breasts and big doe eyes, which he knew would make her popular with the male customers. And she had waitressing experience, having worked at a well-known local restaurant, *The Daily Catch*, which specialized in seafood, particularly oysters and crabs trucked in daily from fishermen who worked the waters of the Chesapeake Bay.

The type of restaurant didn't matter to Charlie. What mattered was that *The Daily Catch* was always busy, which meant that Chloe was used to juggling many orders at once.

When he told her that she probably wouldn't get the same level of tips, she just shook her head and said it didn't matter. She was looking for a fresh start, away from "certain people" who'd been giving her a hard time at *The Daily Catch.*

Charlie signed her up on the spot.

Demetria "Dee" Wilson, a polar opposite to the quiet, demure Chloe, was a chatterbox-philosopher with the ability to uplift your spirits while recounting every dark corner of her life. A single mother who had been beaten, on occasion, "to within an inch of my life" by her "no-good bastard" of a husband, now long absent, "detoxin' somewhere or dead in a ditch," she remained optimistic about the future.

"But you know how it can get sometimes, Mr. Brace, being married yourself," she said, pointing at his wedding ring.

"Oh, actually, no. My wife is gone."

"Left you, like my stinkin' husband?"

"No, she died.

Dee put her hand over her mouth and shook her head. "Oh, I'm so sorry. Me and my big mouth."

Charlie held a hand up. "No, no, what else were you to think. It's been three years; I just can't seem to put the ring aside, is all.

"I just—"

"Meant no harm, I'm sure."

"Right, right," She said and then changed the subject. "So what I meant to say is that a person has to be resilient in the face of what life dishes up, you know?"

"Yes, I know what you mean."

As evidence of her resilience, she undid the top button to her blouse, pulling the cloth aside to reveal a large scar, a knife wound across the top of her left breast.

"But it's just a scar, see."

See? Charlie could barely look away.

"Life deals out pain, Mr. Brace, but you can make it a *gain* if you just try. And I owe it to Pearl to try."

"Pearl?" Charlie knew she meant her daughter, but he was so distracted by her energy and beauty—her hand still clutched at her blouse, her breast half exposed, her skin otherwise smooth and cocoa brown—he didn't know what else to say.

"My daughter," she said dropping her hand away, breaking his reverie, forcing him to look at her face. Here, too, he became lost in her features. If ever eyes could be said to twinkle, hers surely did. They were large and round and golden brown and seemed to see in him something if not amusing, then at least interesting. Her nose was thin, her lips full, her smile disarming. He could not look away.

"Right, right, your daughter."

She smiled at him. "Look at me, I've been talkin' my head off and not getting to the point, which of course is, I need a job, Mr. Brace."

Charlie extended his hand across the booth. "Then you shall have a job, Mrs. Wilson."

She clapped her hands together, then shook his hand vigorously, smiling broadly. "You won't regret this, sir, you won't."

Charlie knew he wouldn't.

Monroe Brown, late of the dining hall at the nearby Jessup Correctional Center, looking for a fresh start in front of The Red Oak's grills and fryers, was as big and menacing looking as a linebacker, but with a booming laugh that could only be described as jolly. Everything great and small was a source of head-shaking wonderment and amusement to him, from his crime—stealing a box of candy for his mother's birthday—to his punishment: ten years hard.

Whatever his past, he knew his way around a stovetop and was blessed with a photographic memory, a blessing that would reap many benefits when the Sunday crowd poured in looking for a little more than a communion wafer and a jigger of grape juice.

But it was his laugh that turned out to be the real blessing, creating an ambience so friendly that even the most pinch-faced customers had to soften and smile, to forget at least for a time, whatever problems they carried into the diner and to yield to the healing sermon of a joyous laugh.

Jimmy "Deuce" Smith, a former high school jock with biceps as big as sweet potatoes, which he took great pride in displaying, was just looking for a job—anything—to put some cash in his pockets while he tried to decide what to do next. College was out—he couldn't afford it and was too undersized to play quarterback—but he had not yet resigned himself to a workaday life. Some miracle would surely come along to vault him to a life of indolent luxury and fast women, free from all care. Or so he thought.

His only question for Charlie had nothing to do with the job. "Do you work out?"

Charlie shook his head.

"You can probably tell I do." He held up his right arm and flexed his bicep repeatedly. "Free weights, it's the only way. I can give you some tips to turn those ropes of yours into guns."

"Interesting," Charlie said, but then changed the subject. "So what are your long-range plans?"

Deuce seemed disappointed by this turn, but then shrugged. "Well, I may travel some, maybe live in France."

He said this with a wink and a sidelong, leering smile at Chloe, who was standing with Dee near the counter, comparing notes on their new jobs. Chloe caught the look, smiled demurely, and nervously turned away, grabbing Dee by the elbow and moving her down the counter away from Charlie and Deuce.

Charlie did his best to suppress a smile, not wanting to throw cold water on the boy's plans, for Chloe or France, however unattainable each seemed.

"Well, busing tables would be a start."

"Okay, then, when do I start?"

Apparently, the tug of France—or Chloe—was strong.

Jesus Alvear, a slight, diminutive man with slicked-back black hair that reminded Charlie of Grace Sharp's lawyer, what's-his-name, had shark-black eyes that seemed to be ever lost in sadness and prayer. But when he sat down opposite Charlie and clicked open the long leather case he had brought with him, Charlie knew one of *his* prayers had been answered. Jesus was an angel.

The case, lined in blue velvet, contained a gleaming assortment of knives, long and short.

"German steel," he said, his Spanish accent so thick and heavy Charlie half expected the words to drop from his mouth like marbles and skitter away. "The finest."

Charlie could think of only one response. "Wow."

Jesus smiled, the sadness briefly disappearing from his eyes. "I know you probably have your own knives, sir, but these are the tools of my trade."

"No-no, that's fine," Charlie said, nodding vigorously. "You can use your own knives—they look great."

Jesus considered this. "Good, that is good, but . . ."

"Yes, what is it?"

Jesus rested his arms on the table and leaned in, his eyes fixed on Charlie's. "Sir, may I ask *you* a question?"

"Of course, shoot."

"What is the *secret* of a good sandwich?"

Charlie didn't give the question much thought. "Well, let me see, I guess I would say the meat or the bread. Oh, and maybe the lettuce—it has to be fresh and crisp . . ."

Jesus held up a hand to silence him.

"No, no, sir, it is the *cut*."

"Oh, I see. You mean straight across or diagonal?"

Jesus grimaced, shaking his head. "No, sir, no . . . I mean the *quality* of the cut, the *fineness* of the cut."

"Ah, the knife."

Jesus scowled at him like a teacher frustrated with a poor student. "The knife is important, yes. Its weight, length, shape, and sharpness—all, all are important—but it is the man *behind* the knife . . ."

"The angel."

The word startled Jesus. "Ah, I see you know the lingo. That is good. And yes, it is the angel, the man who must play the sandwich like a violin . . ."

Charlie almost burst out laughing, nearly overcome by the image of Jesus at work, an uncut sandwich tucked under his chin, draped across his shoulder, his knife poised above the bread like a bow.

"Of course, the angel," Charlie said, unable to suppress a smile, a smile that was not lost on Jesus, who wagged a finger at him.

"I can see you think this is amusing, sir, but I assure you it is nothing less than serious, serious business."

Charlie did his best to recover. "No, no, I can see that," he said. "Forgive me. I just had this image in my head . . ."

Jesus held up a hand again, stopping Charlie cold. "Think about it, sir, the knife slicing first through the bread, then the lettuce, the tomato, each with their own textures, then deeper still the meat, again with its own thickness and texture, and finally the bread again, but *not* the bread again."

"Not?"

"No, the bottom slice, remember, has been coated uniformly with mustard or—god forbid—mayonnaise, and that changes *everything*."

Charlie looked at him blankly.

"Don't you see, sir? It is not just a matter of slicing through the sandwich with a sharp knife—anyone can do *that*."

"Right, I can see that."

Jesus shook his head dismissively. "No, I don't think you do. You see, what has to happen is that the knife must pass through all these layers *just so*: lightly, slowly through the bread, a little more quickly but in one smooth draw of the knife through the lettuce and tomato, then a quick sawing action through the meat, but not too quick or forceful—you don't want to compress the bread below—and finally a light, single stroke through the mustard-coated bread. Just so, just so, just so, just so—you see? It is like making love to a woman, and it is my art."

And with that he slumped back in the booth, waiting for Charlie to respond.

What do you say to an angel? Charlie said, "You're hired."

Three hours later, Charlie's search for help was nearly complete. He needed another waitress but was dead-set on Jeanie Beene—he'd just have to get that recipe from Grace Sharp, then lure Jeanie back with the best mud in town.

He also needed one more busboy to go along with Deuce and the two other busboys he'd hired, both named Lenny, both pleased but not thrilled with the opportunity. That search ended when *Sarah Walters* near dragged her son, *Paulie*, into the diner.

"My son here is too shy to ask, Mr. Brace, but he's a good boy and a hard worker. Ask him once and he'll get the job done. Ask him twice and you'll never have to ask again—he'll see to it that it's done, and done well."

Charlie smiled at her and turned to Paulie, who stood behind her, head down, nervously rocking from one foot to the other. He was tall and gangly, with the kind of broad, long-fingered hands that basketball coaches dream about. But there was an awkwardness about him, a clumsiness that would have turned every coach away. His blond hair, dark as Dijon mustard, was bowl-cut, probably by his mother, giving him a lean Friar Tuck look.

"What do you think, Paulie? I have one position left, for a busboy."

Paulie stopped rocking and glanced up at him. There was something odd about his eyes. Whether it was their color, a blue as pale as the sky in winter, or the way they fixed on Charlie like a hawk's on prey, the effect was chilling. Charlie had the feeling that another person—stronger, more confident, and dangerous—was behind those eyes, struggling to get out.

"'kay," he said, "'kay." His voice was deep and dry, with the rasp of extended silence.

Charlie extended his hand to welcome him to the team, but Paulie stepped back behind his mother, who quickly extended her own hand. "Thank you, Mr. Brace. Thank you."

"No problem. Make sure Paulie is here tomorrow morning at seven sharp," he said, escorting them to the door and out through the foyer to their car, a classic '57 Chevy in what appeared to be excellent condition.

"Wow, nice car," Charlie offered.

"My husband's hobby, I'm afraid. Thanks again, Mr. Brace." She and Paulie got into the car, slowly backed out of their spot, and edged out onto the highway. Charlie watched them head up toward the college, crest the hill, and disappear.

When he turned to go back into the diner, he noticed the column of smoke in the trees again. *Could it really be the same guy?* he thought. He decided to investigate, trudging across the parking lot and making his way through brambles and underbrush toward the spot where he thought he'd find the man and his campfire. But by the time he had taken fifty steps into the woods, the smoke had vanished. He stood quietly for a few moments, listening for any twig snap or other noise that might point him in the right direction, but the woods were silent as a grave.

That night, he dreamed about his wife, Lara, part of the same dream he always had about her, the car flipping into the air and rolling down the hill, the two of them tossed about like rag dolls. The pain. The blood. The metallic crunching sounds that never seemed to end as the car rolled and rolled, seemingly in slow motion, finally slamming into a tree, throwing Charlie clear and trapping Lara inside, her door jammed. Charlie staggering to his feet, gagging on the smell of gasoline. The look on Lara's face as she pounded on the window, screaming his name. And then the explosion, Charlie blasted into the air, thrown on his back, knocking the breath from him, ears ringing.
And then silence.

Sometimes the dream would start earlier, during the argument they were having just before she lost control of the car, or earlier still, at the party that had set things in motion.

And sometimes, like tonight, the dream would startle him awake, and Lara would be standing in the shadows near the bed, staring down at him.

CHAPTER 6

CHARLIE COULD TELL FROM HER VOICE, the dreaminess of it, the *hello* seemingly coming from some far off place, that he had awakened her. "Oh, I'm sorry," he said. "I didn't mean to wake you up."

"Minute," she said. There was a long pause. He could hear covers being thrown back, a lamp switched on, and a barely stifled yawn. He imagined her sitting on the edge of the bed in a negligee, legs crossed, one hand pulling the hair back from her face, the other lifting the phone back to her ear. "Yes?" she said, her voice near normal now. "Who is it?"

He should never have called so early on a Sunday, but he couldn't hang up now.

"It's Charlie Brace, ma'am, the guy who bought your diner."

"What's *happened?*" The alarm in her voice caught Charlie by surprise.

"What?"

"Has something *happened* . . . at the diner?"

Charlie had no idea where she was going with this. "The diner? No, everything is fine. I was just calling to ask for a favor, is all."

She sighed heavily into the phone. "Whew, a *favor?* I thought, well . . . never mind what I thought. I've been under a lot of stress lately and—"

"No problem, and please, call me Charlie."

There was a pause.

"And me, *Grace*," she said, her voice suddenly softer. "Or Gracie . . . Charlie."

Some say that love begins when a person first says your name, that it is as telling as your first sight of them or your first kiss. If you had asked Charlie point-blank, right then and there, what he thought of that proposition, he would have no doubt laughed and said, "What a load of crap."

But now, in the moment, he just laughed. "I think I'll go with Grace. Gracie always reminds me of George Burns and Gracie Allen, and you are *so* not her."

She returned the laugh, hers deep and lusty. Charlie imagined her head thrown back, the arch of her neck, a strap falling off her shoulder.

"Bill would have disagreed with you. He would say I'm *exactly* like Gracie."

"Sorry," he said. "I just don't see that." Charlie could sense from her silence that he had perhaps said the wrong thing . . . or the very right thing.

"Are you *flirting* with me, Charlie?"

"Um . . ."

She giggled. "Just teasing, a woman my age, but I'll *definitely* take that as a compliment. Anyway, what's so important at 7:30 on a Sunday morning?"

"Wow, I feel stupid asking now."

"No, no, really, it's all right. I should have been up by now."

"Well, it's about your coffee recipe."

"Oh," she said, clearly disappointed, her voice a lesson in flatness, in monotone. "Hold on."

He could hear her footsteps as she padded barefoot across the room, opened a dresser drawer, fumbled with some papers, and returned to the bed, the box spring creaking.

"Okay," she said, finally. "Got a pencil and paper?"

"Yes, go ahead, shoot."

He had expected her to launch into a description of various coffee beans—Arabican, Ethiopian, Sumatran, Columbian, Zambian, and the like—how they should be ground, blended, and roasted, the specific equipment needed and their costs, and where he could find everything he'd need to brew the best coffee on the planet.

Nothing could have prepared him for what she actually said next.

"Okay, you start with a pound of Meyer's Black Label . . ."

"*Meyers?*"

"Yes, have you heard of it?"

"Yeah, but everyone says Meyers is bad."

"Yes, exactly, but it's cheap and, more important, it's what most restaurants use."

"I don't get it."

"Listen," she said, "sooner or later, your competition is going to find out what you're serving, and if they think you're serving Meyers Black Label, so much the better. They'll relax because it's exactly what they're serving."

"No, no, what I mean is, why are we even *using* it?"

"I just told you."

"Yes, I know, but I'm told it tastes, well, nasty."

"Listen," she said, growing impatient, "do you want the formula, or what?"

"Okay, sorry, what's next?"

She fumbled with the paper. "Let me see, where was I . . . yes. To the Meyers add one cup of Maxwell House, one cup of Yuban, and a half-cup of any ground espresso you can find—even instant will do in a pinch. Mix it all up, and that's it."

"Really?"

"Yeah, you can't miss. Oh, and one other thing. Name it after the prettiest waitress you've got."

"Huh?"

"I know it sounds silly, but hey, the sizzle is just as important as the steak. Trust me, the coffee will taste even better, especially to your male customers, if they think a pretty woman made it for them."

It did sound silly to Charlie. "Okay . . . well, thanks, Grace, I appreciate the tip and—"

She sensed he was about to end the call. "Whoa, not so fast, mister, there's more."

"More?"

"Yeah, who's your prettiest waitress?"

Charlie's first thought was Dee, who had filled his thoughts ever since the interview. He could hardly wait to see her again. But when he put on his owner-proprietor hat and tried his best to be objective, the result was a tie: Chloe was equally pretty.

"Actually, I've got two pretty waitresses."

"Hmm. Okay, let's break the tie. Close your eyes and picture each of them standing before you naked, holding up a cup of steaming coffee for you."

"Whoa, I don't think—"

"Exactly, *don't* think. Just picture them. Come on, this is important."

Charlie closed his eyes and considered them. Chloe of the alabaster skin and large breasts. Doe-eyed Chloe, long-legged Chloe. And then Dee of the satin brown skin and full lips. Golden-eyed Dee and her disarming smile.

"Well?" Grace said.

"I'm not sure, they're both beautiful."

Grace giggled. "Such a gentleman. Let me make it easy for you. Which one has the biggest tits?"

Charlie could not contain the laugh that burst from him. "That would be Chloe—*definitely*."

"Perfect. You'll call the coffee *Chloe's Joe.*"

"Um, but she pronounces it Chlo-ee, not Chlo."

"Doesn't matter. Whether it's *Chloe's Jo* or *Chlo-ee's Jo-ee*, as long as she's got big tits . . ."

"Gotcha. Okay, I'll give it a try."

"Good, well . . . I guess that's it, then?"

"No, wait, a couple of things."

"Okay." She sounded relieved that the call wasn't ending.

"I'd like you to come down for the grand opening next Saturday."

The tone in her voice changed quickly. The idea did not appeal to her. "To the diner? Well, I'd like to,

I really would, but the diner is something I'd sooner forget."

"Are you sure? I'd really like to show you what I've done to her."

"Well . . ."

"Come on, it'll be fun."

His appeal was met with a long silence.

"Grace?"

"Sorry, Charlie, just thinking."

"Don't think. Come."

"I'll give it some thought, I really will, but it's hard for me, you know?"

"Your husband?"

"Yeah, and other things, too, but look, let's just leave it at *maybe*."

"Okay, but I hope you'll change your mind."

She needed to change the subject. "So, you said there were a *couple* of things. What else?"

"Oh, that. I was just curious . . ."

"Yeah? About what?"

"What you called *your* coffee." He could tell she was smiling on the other end of the line.

"We called it *Gracie's*, Charlie. Can you picture that?"

CHAPTER 7

THE DAYS BEFORE THE GRAND OPENING were even busier than all the days that had gone before. Menus were finalized and duplicated, uniforms chosen and fitted, details large and small dealt with and checked off a list that Charlie carried around with him on a clipboard. And then there was the matter of Jeanie Beene.

She was reluctant at first to even come back for a second interview, but after Charlie assured her that he'd changed the coffee for the better, she relented.

Charlie had paced the diner all morning, occasionally going out to the road to see if he could spot her car, an old Buick, the maroon paint faded to grayish silver on the hood, where engine heat and the elements had done their destructive dance.

But she was so late now he began to wonder whether he was looking in the right direction, or whether she would ever come at all, so he stood there, hands on hips, looking first to the west, where he thought her car would appear, then to the east, his head on a swivel. After twenty minutes, all he had seen was a steady stream of cars and trucks, none a Buick, and now, far off toward the west, two figures, one tall, one short, a woman and a child, walking along the shoulder, headed in his direction, each carrying what looked like a wicker basket, the child shifting hers from hand to hand, long-armed from the weight of whatever lay within.

Charlie heard a buzzing sound behind him and turned to see the R in the DINER sign flickering. And then the R was fine, but the D began flickering. And then all the letters started flickering and flashing at random. It reminded him of the flashing lights on the alien mothership in *Close Encounters of the Third Kind*.

He punched in the number of Neon Discounters and left a message for Larry. *This has got to be fixed!*

And then he looked up and there she was, barreling down the road toward him. Charlie gave her a wave as she turned into the lot and rumbled to a gravel-spraying stop at the diner's entrance. She climbed out of the car without a word, shook her head at the flickering signs, and accompanied Charlie inside, not even replying to his overly cheery "mornin'!"

She got right to it, asking for a cup of coffee without so much as taking off her coat. Clearly, if the coffee wasn't right, she'd be "outta here."

Charlie poured her a mug, handed it to her, held his breath, and watched as she raised it tentatively to her lips and took a sip.

"My," she said, her eyes widening. She took another sip. "My, my, *my*."

She held the mug out in front of her, smiling, considering the color, the smell of the steaming coffee.

"Mr. Brace, this is, this is . . . *wonderful.*"

"You like it?"

"Oh, my, yes. When word gets around about this—and it *will* get around if *I* have anything to say about it—you'll have to beat the customers away with a stick. What brand is it, anyway?"

"Not a brand," Charlie said. "A secret formula."

"You don't say. Well, congratulations to the genius who came up with it. Whatcha call it?"

Halfway through his saying "Chloe's Joe" her brow furrowed and her smile disappeared. *Oh, no,* Charlie thought, *she can't be thinking "Jeanie's Beanies" can she?*

Charlie pointed to Chloe standing behind the counter. She had the new uniform on, which emphasized her figure. "That's Chloe," he said.

Jeanie's reaction was instant and wholly unexpected. "Ha! Now *that* is genius," she laughed. "How did you know to do that?"

He started to reply, but she stopped him.

"Never mind, it's perfect, just perfect."

"So . . . does that mean?"

"Oh, absolutely, Mr. Brace. I'd be happy to work here, no doubt."

"Great!" Charlie threw an arm around her shoulders and led her to the center of the diner. "Listen up, everybody. Say hello to our new waitress, Jeanie Beene."

The others briefly stopped what they were doing, gave Jeanie a smile, a nod, and a polite wave, and then went back to work, each self-absorbed in the tasks, the details, that would bring the diner to life.

Charlie turned back to Jeanie. "See Dee over there for your uniforms and if you need additional fitting,

I've made a deal with Sarah Kim at So-Kleen down the street."

"Okay, I know Sarah; she'll do a good job."

"Well then, the grand opening is Saturday, but we'll do a soft opening on Wednesday, day after tomorrow. That'll give us a few days to get our act together before the weekend."

"Sounds good to me," Jeanie said. "When do you want me here."

"Two hours before opening, about five, if that's okay?"

"With bells on, Mr. Brace, with bells on." She turned to go, then stopped and turned back to him.

"A couple of things . . ."

"Yeah?"

"You're gonna fix those neon signs, right?"

"Oh, yes. I've already called the sign company to come fix them.'

"Well, good, 'cause we don't want to appear shabby and second-rate."

"No, of course not," Charlie said. "And the second thing?"

"Your pies," she said, a look of deep concern on her face. "Who's supplyin' them?"

"Consolidated Bakery, out in Dundalk."

Jeanie frowned. "They'll do, I guess, but you should probably steer clear of their Magoo."

"Magoo? Magoo? You mean the apple pie?"

"Custard," she said, giving him a look that said *you are totally hopeless*. "It has this metallic aftertaste. We'll just have to hope Chloe's Joe saves the day."

"Well, look, is there a better supplier?"

Jeanie shook her head. "Not really. All of them big bakeries tend toward the industrial. No, what you need is some local housewife with a decent oven, time on her hands, and her grandma's recipes."

"Maybe I could put an ad in the paper."

"Maybe, but my experience is, if there's someone out there, they'll find you. Time will tell."

CHAPTER 8

THEY SAY THAT MOST THINGS IN LIFE are a matter of timing, and whether through the clockwork machinations of fate, or pure serendipity, such was this moment.

Two figures, one tall, one short, one a woman, one a child, had pushed into the diner, carrying with them, in baskets creaking from the cold, the unmistakable aroma of fresh-baked pie.

The first thing Jeanie noticed about them was their clothes. The woman wore a yellow gingham dress and a matching light sweater, its sleeves pushed up to her elbows—perfectly normal for spring, but hardly adequate for the wind-whipped chill of this October morning, and clearly a dress that had been worn several days running.

And when she looked at the little girl and how she was dressed—dirty jeans overalls and a short-sleeved red jersey—an admonishing *tch-tch-tch* began to form in her throat, held back only by a politeness too weak to stand much more. Jeanie bit her lip and tried her best to smile.

Charlie, like any man, noticed the woman's clothes only insofar as they obscured or revealed her figure, which in this case was of a woman rail-thin, all elbows and knees and angles, with only the slightest hint of breasts, made evident by the morning's chill. Hollow-cheeked and sallow, slate-blue eyes sunken and dark-rimmed, hair drawn back severely into a mud-brown ponytail, she appeared to have risen from her sickbed.

The little girl, frail like her mother and no more than ten years old by Charlie's reckoning, stood behind the woman, clinging to her dress, peering up at Charlie with large round eyes that at once evoked sadness, a catlike wariness, and a world-weariness far beyond her years. She had her mother's nose, long and thin, but the shape of her face, rounder and flatter, and the fullness of her lips suggested a father's seminal influence, as did her curly black hair, so tousled it resembled steel wool.

Charlie felt the need to put the little girl at ease, so he bent down and addressed her first. "Don't worry, I don't bite," he said, giving her a smile so broad it bordered on the theatrical.

This seemed to suggest to the girl that the opposite was true. She retreated further behind her mother.

"She's a little shy," the mother said. "Mindy, say hello." Her voice was high-pitched, almost childlike, with a pronounced lisp.

Mindy peered around her again and offered a quick hello in a voice deeper and considerably more adult than her mother's.

The mother offered a thin-lipped smile and extended her hand. "I'm Martha."

Charlie took her hand and squeezed it gently. The hand was neither cold nor warm but appeared to Charlie so fragile—like holding a baby bird—that a firmer grip would have broken every bone. "Charlie

Brace," he said, "and this is Jeanie Beene, my head waitress."

Martha nodded at Jeanie and then hoisted her basket, a pie holder, onto the nearest table. "I bake pies," she said, turning to grab Mindy's basket, placing it next to hers. She threw back the lids and unloaded the pies, announcing each as she lifted them out. "Apple . . . peach . . . custard . . . banana cream . . . I can do others, whatever you like: cherry, lemon meringue, pumpkin, coconut cream, you name it."

"Let's have a taste," Jeanie said, moving behind the counter to collect plates, forks, and a knife.

Martha took the knife and served up thin wedges of each pie for Charlie and Jeanie. Charlie was won over by his first bite of apple pie, offering up a "wow" that made Martha beam. Jeanie was more methodical and noncommittal until she had tasted each, taking time between bites to clear her palate with a sip of Chloe's Joe; then she gave Charlie a nod and Martha a wink.

"*Lord*, girl, where have *you* been hidin' in this town?"

Charlie chimed in. "Yeah, these are great. We'll need, what, six pies a day, Jeanie?"

"No, sir, I'd say eight, two each of the apple and custard, one each of the peach, lemon meringue, cherry, and chocolate cream. You can do all those, right?"

Martha nodded vigorously. "Oh, yes."

"And we'll need them early each morning," Charlie said.

"Before seven," Jeanie added.

"We can do that, can't we Mindy?"

Mindy nodded half-heartedly, as if the thought of waking so early, let alone helping her mother bake eight pies a day, was far from joyful.

"Okay, then," Charlie said. "About the price . . ."

"Whatever you think is fair, Mr. Brace, but I use the finest ingredients—real butter and cream, fresh fruit—so I was hoping for at least five dollars a pie—and an advance on the fist order."

Consolidated Bakery was going to charge him no more than three dollars a pie, but he could see from the way Jeanie was nodding that the pies would be worth every penny.

He extended his hand to Martha again. "It looks like we're in the pie business, Martha."

She took his hand and shook it firmly, her eyes fixed on his. "Thank you!"

CHAPTER 9

Twenty minutes after Martha, Mindy, and Jeanie had left the diner, the Neon Discounts van came rumbling into the parking lot. Charlie peered out the window and watched as Larry got out of the van, looked up at the sign, and lifted both arms, hands palms up as if to say, "What gives?"

Charlie took off his apron and headed out to greet him. "Glad you could come so quickly. Having trouble with the signs."

"What kind of trouble?" said Larry, pointing up at the Red Oak Diner sign. "Looks okay to me."

Charlie turned around and looked up. The sign was functioning perfectly. Not so much as a single flicker or buzz.

"That's odd," Charlie said. "It was buzzing and flickering like mad just half an hour ago."

"Humph," said Larry, tugging at his tool belt as if he were a gunslinger adjusting his holsters. He was a small man, thin and wiry, with a pink complexion that suggested heavy drinking, a suggestion that showed up in his bloodshot eyes as well. His face was thin, almost ferret-like. Red hair, pulled back into a ponytail and mostly hidden under a John Deere cap, matched a goatee badly in need of a trim. He chewed on a mint that did little to cover up his whiskey breath.

"Humph," he repeated. "Is that so?"

"Yeah, it was like something out of *Close Encounters of the Third Kind.* You know, when the mother ship flashes its lights like crazy?"

Larry gave him a blank look.

"It's a movie. You must have seen it. You know, the one where Richard Dreyfus sculpts this mountain, or maybe it was a butte, out of mashed potatoes."

Larry shook his head. "Must have missed that one." He looked up at the sign again. "Anyway, were the letters all flashing at once?"

"No, it started with the letter R, but then spread to the other letters, and they were like flickering independent of one another. And no real pattern to it, either."

"No pattern?"

"No, seemed pretty random, but the flickering was really fast, really intense."

Larry spit out what remained of the mint. "But now it's fine." It was more of a statement than a question.

"Yes, I guess, but could you check it out, anyway?"

Larry pursed his lips and shook his head. "If it's workin', it's workin'. Only thing it could be, way you describe it, is one of two things.

"What two things?"

"Well, it could be an intermittent short-circuit, maybe in the diner's wiring, not the sign's."

Charlie shook his head. "That seems very unlikely. I had all the electrical replaced, even put in a new circuit box. And it's all been inspected and certified by the county."

"Well then," Larry mused, "it can only be one other thing."

"Okay, what?"

"This here diner is an alien mothership."

And with that, Larry tipped his hat, climbed back into the van, and started it up. "You call me if it flickers again," he said, leaning his head out the window and giving Charlie a wink.

He accelerated out of the parking lot and headed up the hill toward the college.

In the dream, Charlie and Lara were arguing about who should drive home from the party, Lara pointing out, correctly, that Charlie was "drunk as hell," and she wasn't about to let him drive.

Charlie finally relented and climbed into the front passenger seat, turning with a start when he heard Dee's voice.

"What's this all about, Charlie?" she said from the back seat. "Me and Chloe and Jeanie want to know."

Charlie started to respond but was interrupted by Lara. "If you ever *embarrass me like that again, this marriage is over!"*

Charlie screamed at her. "Me? Me embarrassing you? The way you fawned and cooed over Richard, practically sucked his cock right in front of everyone. Now that *was embarrassing."*

"I did no such thing and you know it."

Charlie screamed at her. "Just shut up!"

Charlie heard a chorus of gasps coming from the back seat. Jeanie and Chloe were now in the car, sitting with Dee.

"Tch-tch-tch," said Jeanie, shaking her head disapprovingly. "I don't like the looks of this."

"Stop looking at my tits, Charlie!" shouted Chloe.

"Charlie, what's this all about?" Dee pleaded.

Charlie turned and looked at her. "It's about this."

He turned, looked at Lara, and passed out, his head slamming into her arm. The car began to swerve as Lara lost control.

CHAPTER 10

THE SOFT OPENING PROVED TO BE HARDER than anyone had expected. It reminded Charlie of his first abortive dance lesson, the one his mother had dragged him to, at age ten, part of her master plan for turning her scab-kneed son into someone who could pass for civilized, at least for the length of a song. He had stepped on his partner's toes, twisted her left when the step called for right, failed to find the beat in the music, and generally presented an image aptly described by the dance teacher, a reed-thin, long-necked woman who could have patented the smirk, as "herky-jerky."

So too the diner staff. Waitresses collided in the close quarters behind the counter, spilling coffee and food. Busboys miscalculated their loads and lost their balance, greatly diminishing the supply of dishes. Cooks were, as Jeanie put it, "in the weeds," serving up food too late or out of sequence, leaving customers with cold hot-roast-beef sandwiches or nothing at all.

But several things kept the customers from bolting. Chloe's Joe was an instant hit, as was she, the men following her every move, smiling at her as she approached, leering at her as she passed, shaking their heads in awe, relishing their great good fortune to be sitting here, at this very moment, in the presence of a goddess; Dee Wilson, herself no less a goddess and as outgoing as Chloe was demure, engaged each customer, smiling at them, winking, flirting, making them hers with "honeys" and "darlin's" and a level of attention bordering on sexual, the men lapping her up as hungrily as they did Monroe Brown's gravy; Monroe Brown himself, laughing at every dropped plate, every miscue great or small, made the customers feel that they were not watching a disaster but participating in some folly, some theatrical farce, contrived for their amusement; and Jeanie Beene, talking in what sounded like tongues, left the customer's drop-jawed and laughing about what they had just ordered. Coffee with cream and sugar became "a blonde with sand" on Jeanie's lips; doughnuts became life preservers; eggs, cackle fruit; butter, cow paste; sausage, a Zeppelin; hamburger, a hockey puck; and on and on, delighting the customers and confounding Monroe and the short-order cooks, who strained to hear, let alone translate, the orders over the clatter of the dishes and the hiss of the grill.

By Friday, though, three days into it, the diner and its staff were dancing with the grace of Fred Astaire and Ginger Rogers, despite the fact that the number of customers had increased three-fold since the Wednesday opening, word-of-mouth praise spreading through the town as rapidly and surely as the flu. And the now constantly flickering signs seemed to make little difference.

They had become a team. Well, almost a team, Monroe and Jesus, while working well with everyone else, seemed to be at each other from day one, as if they were in some kind of trash-talking competition, about what, Charlie couldn't imagine. Not that they were loud or distracting. They seemed to communicate in whispers and pointed fingers. He would have to have a talk with them.

Still, all this left Charlie smiling, and exhausted. He had never imagined how much work would be involved, how myriad the details, how fine the line between order and chaos. But he was pleased nonetheless, and eager to see what tomorrow would bring.

For now, though, hours after the dinner rush, he contented himself by taking out the accumulated trash and garbage and tossing it into the dumpster out back. The evening was clear and crisp, his breath coming now in steamy puffs, the sky starry, the moon bright orange, hanging low in the sky just above the tree line. And he was alone, peacefully alone.

Or so he thought.

"Some might call that a Harvest Moon, you know," a voice behind him said. "Of course, they'd be wrong."

Charlie recognized the voice immediately. "Well, hello again. I see you found me."

"Not that difficult if you have a nose for diners; besides, you told me where to look."

"So, would you like to take a look inside, see how I fixed her up?"

The man backed away a few steps. "Some other time, perhaps. I'm enjoying this moon too much. Not a Harvest Moon, of course. That was last month, of course, first full moon following the autumnal equinox. This here's different—all sorts of atmospheric shit going on, light playing tricks on us, reflecting and refracting, twisted like a dishcloth by a pissed-off housewife, if you get me. And besides, it's not even full."

Charlie didn't know what to say next. "You seem to know a lot about the moon."

"Been watching it wax and wane longer than you've been alive. Some might mistake this one for a Vulcan Moon, but that's a rare event; moon turns blood red, no mistakin' it."

Charlie was torn between the desire to end this conversation and an innate curiosity about a man that by any definition would have been considered a curiosity.

"Ah," the man said. "I see you're a bit put off by my appearance, but I'd appreciate it if you'd stop staring at me like a cow at a new fence."

Charlie laughed despite himself. "Sorry, you just startled me, is all . . . but I have to ask what you're doing back here *behind* my diner. Could have just come in the front."

"I guess you might call me an *independent food critic*. Used to be a diner man myself." He held up a partially eaten cheeseburger. "Take this, for example. Looks like a cheeseburger, hefts like a cheeseburger, has something yellow on top, maybe cheese, but something tells me it's not very good." He stopped and waggled the cheeseburger.

"Why's that?" Charlie said, intrigued. "Does it taste bad?"

"Haven't tasted it yet."

"Then how—"

"Evidence," he said, holding up his sack. "I'd say fifteen half-eaten cheeseburgers pretty much says it all. Good news for me, bad news for you."

The man offered Charlie the cheeseburger. "Here, have a taste."

Charlie waved him off, grimacing. "No, thanks." He had had too many run-ins with the maggots that lived in the dumpster, what his mother called "moving rice," an expression that kept him out of Chinese restaurants for years.

The man laughed and took a bite of the cheeseburger, a look of disgust growing on his face as he chewed and, with what seemed great difficulty, swallowed. "Oh, man," he said, "that's nasty."

"What's wrong?"

"Two things: the meat's overcooked—dry as a bone—and the cheese is only partially melted, and pretty skimpy, I might add."

"So cook it less and make sure the cheese is melted?"

"And more of it. Oh, and the roll's too big. The burger should flop out all around. Makes the customer think he's getting more for his money. *More* trumps *taste* every time. Curious thing, greed, but the cornerstone of capitalism."

"Well," Charlie said, trying to wrap up this conversation, "thanks for the tips. I've gotta get back inside now. Good seeing you again."

The man held out his hand. "Didn't really introduce myself last time. Name's Heph, Heph Marshall, late of Connecticut, on the road many a year now."

Charlie reluctantly took his hand, which was cold and leathery and a bit greasy from his foray into the dumpster. "Charlie Brace, late of right here."

"So, can you guess why I'm called Heph?"

Charlie shook his head and shrugged. "No idea."

"After Hephaestus, the Greek god of fire and the forge. Roman's called him Vulcan."

"Interesting."

"Yeah . . . but know why my parents named me Hephaestus? Let me tell you, that's quite a name to take to school."

"I guess they were into mythology."

"Yes, true enough, but mostly it was because I was born with one leg considerably shorter than the other."

"So?"

"The myth is that Vulcan's father, Jupiter, the head man, threw Vulcan from the heavens during a fight with the boy's mom, Juno. Vulcan landed so hard that one leg ended up shorter than the other."

"Humph. Really?"

"Yeah, of course, there's another version that blames Juno entirely. In that one, Juno is so aghast at the sight of the new-born Vulcan that she flings him off Olympus."

"Interesting," Charlie said, half-heartedly, barely resisting the temptation to look at his watch.

"Yeah, makes you wonder about those cultures, don't it?"

Charlie shrugged, giving him a blank look.

"I mean," Heph continued, "the Romans blamed the father, the Greeks the mother. What's with that?"

"Dunno." Charlie glanced at his watch. 11:45. He had to get back inside to see how the cleanup was going.

"Me neither. Of course, given *my* parents, I'd say both myths pretty much hit the mark." He grew silent, averting his eyes to gaze off toward the waiting darkness of the woods. "Anyway, enough of that. Time's a wastin', for me and for you it seems."

He picked up his sack, slung it over his shoulder, and gave Charlie a little two-fingered salute. "'night then."

"'night," Charlie said.

With that, Heph turned and walked away, disappearing into the trees, the sound of his footsteps fraying to silence. Charlie stood there staring at the moon, which seemed somehow smaller now, and whiter, no longer in the orange grip of the night.

CHAPTER 11

CHARLIE TOSSED AND TURNED ALL NIGHT, dreams coming, going, overlapping: Charlie riding shotgun in Grace Sharp's pink Cadillac convertible, her dress hitched up to her thighs, her hair whipping in the wind, her eyes focused on him, furtive, imploring, her lips moving rapidly but the words lost in the roar of the engine and the wind; Charlie reaching into Heph's sack on the seat between them and offering her a maggot-riddled cheeseburger, which she gobbled down, licking her lips, asking for more; Martha and little Mindy sitting in the backseat, quietly holding stacks of pies on their laps, Heph sitting between them, laughing and throwing pie after pie over his head into the darkness, the moon blood-red; Charlie making love to Dee, to Chloe, in turn, together, intertwined in the backseat of the speeding car, little Mindy at the wheel reciting nursery rhymes—and the dish ran away with the spoon—*Charlie driving, Grace straddling him, naked, her back against the steering wheel, the horn blaring, a figure suddenly appearing in the headlights*—Lara—*the sound of the horn resolving itself into the familiar tintinnabulation of his alarm clock.*

When he arrived at the diner, everyone was already hard at work getting ready for the grand opening. Martha and Mindy were there, too, unloading a double order of pies from their baskets as Jeanie checked each one off a list.

"Wait, dear," she said to Mindy, "is that a peach or another apple?"

"Apple," Mindy said, absently, her attention focused on Charlie, who gave her a quick smile and a "howdy" before ducking behind the counter to talk to Monroe, who was arguing with the delivery guy from the bakery.

"And I'm tellin' you these here rolls are not ours," he said, tossing a package of rolls back at the man, who was clearly frustrated with Monroe.

"It's okay," Charlie said, intervening. "I special ordered those last night."

Monroe looked at him, incredulous. "Why would you do that, sir? These buns are tiny, won't fit my burgers at all."

"That's the idea, Monroe. Come on outside a minute, I need to talk with you about your cheeseburgers."

"My cheeseburgers? What the—"

"Yeah, come on, grab some coffee and meet me out by the dumpster."

The conversation went well enough, Monroe admitting that overcooking meat was a given in his prison kitchen, where the ground beef arrived smelling of death.

"We called it The Gray Death, sir," he chuckled. "T'weren't nothin' left to do but cook it hard, just to cut the smell some."

Monroe was skeptical about the tiny buns, but agreed to give them a try and see how the customers reacted. So, with visions of cheeseburgers dancing in their heads, Charlie's being greedily eaten by ravenous customers, Monroe's being held between two fingers like a dead mouse, they began to walk back inside. Then Charlie had another thought. "Monroe?"

"Yeah, boss?"

"What is it between you and Jesus?"

Monroe shrugged. "What do you mean?"

"You seem to be on his case all the time."

"Oh, that," Monroe laughed. "Just some friendly trash talkin', is all. Minor disagreements. Nothing to worry yourself about."

Charlie nodded. "Good, good. Well, I guess we better get back inside."

Dee and Chloe greeted Charlie as soon as he stepped through the door, both smiling and energetic, waving rolled up signs in front of his face. Charlie couldn't help thinking about his dream. What would it really be like to make love to them?

"Signs arrived, boss," Dee said.

"So where you want 'em?" said Chloe.

Charlie quickly looked around the diner. "Um, how about the front doors, and then a couple up high above the counter. Do we have tape?"

"Oh, yeah," Chloe said, twirling a roll in front of his face.

"Okay, let's do it then," Dee said. And with that, they were off, Dee heading for the front doors as Chloe scooted behind the counter in search of the small stepladder they used to change light bulbs and the menu board.

Charlie called after her. "Chloe, did the tent signs come, too?"

Before Chloe could answer, Jeanie grabbed one off the counter and tossed it to Charlie.

"They're everywhere, hon. Hardly any room for the customers."

"Oh, we'll make room for *them*," Charlie laughed.

The tent signs, printed in color on glossy card stock and bearing the diner's logo and signature oak leaf, announced two grand opening specials. One side read:

GRAND OPENING SPECIAL!
TODAY ONLY!
FREE COFFEE
ALL DAY!

That was Jeanie's idea. She thought, rightly as it turned out, that Chloe's Joe, and Chloe herself, would be the diner's major draw. So why not give the customers a little taste of the coffee and a drop-jawed gander at Chloe?

The flipside of the tent sign read:
GRAND OPENING SPECIAL!
TODAY ONLY!
FREE PIE
WITH
BREAKFAST COMBO
OR
BLUE-PLATE SPECIAL

This was actually little Mindy's idea, whispered to Charlie on the day she and her mother had delivered the first batch of pies. While her mother and Jeanie were removing the pies from the baskets and sorting them, Mindy slipped into the booth beside Charlie, who was adding up a long column of numbers, a tally of bills to be paid.

"You know," Mindy whispered, "these pies are magical."

Charlie stopped in mid-calculation, dropping his pencil on the table and staring down at Mindy. "Magical?"

Mindy nodded vigorously. "Oh, yes. One bite and—*Shazam!*—you're hooked, under their spell. Nothin' like these pies."

"Shazam," he said flatly. Really?"

"Yes, and you know what?"

"No, what?"

"You want customers coming back, give 'em a free taste. They'll be back, all right. I guarantee it."

"Well," Charlie said in mock-seriousness. "I *like* the idea of a guarantee."

Mindy frowned and slid out of the booth. "Not funny, you'll see." She turned away from him and walked back to the counter, jumping up on a stool near Jeanie and her mother.

That stool was empty now, but wouldn't be for long. The diner would be opening in less than half an hour, and cars were already rolling into the parking lot. Some people stayed in their cars, others lined up at the door, hopping from foot to foot against the cold, giving the doors a tug every few minutes, hoping they'd magically open, that some invisible hand would let them into this world of steaming coffee, smiling faces, and charmed pie. Others pointed up at the sign, where the letter R flickered and buzzed.

And then it was time.

Like puppies scrambling for their mother's teats, the crowd rushed in, each person and family jockeying for just the right stool, just the right booth, Charlie doing his best to seat everyone quickly, Dee and Jeanie swirling around him, a fan of menus in each hand, held high like castanets, while Chloe rushed from cup to cup at the counter, pouring the first taste of Chloe's Joe to men who never took their eyes off her.

Orders were taken, the grill sizzled, and the smell of breakfast filled the air like a heady perfume, Jeanie shouting out the orders, mostly for combos and free pie or just free cups of Chloe's Joe, but a few for off-special breakfasts.

"Adam and Eve on a raft, mystery in the Alley." (Two poached eggs on toast, side order of hash.)

"Blowout patches with a Zeppelin and machine oil." (Pancakes with sausage and syrup.)

"Deadeye, customer will take a chance." (Poached egg with hash.)

"Cackle fruit, wreck 'em, burn the British with a smear." (Scrambled eggs and English muffin with margarine.)

"Short stack with Vermont." (Pancakes with Vermont syrup.)

"Sweep the kitchen, shingle with a shimmy and a shake." (Plate of hash, buttered toast with jelly.)

Monroe laughed his laugh, Jesus's knife flashed and slashed through toast and egg sandwiches, Deuce stood in a corner, flexing his biceps, tray ready, waiting to clear the first table, and Paulie just stood there in the middle of things, oblivious to the people trying to make their way around him, his eyes focused on a trail of smoke curling through the trees outside the diner.

As the hours passed, Charlie grew more and more nervous and anxious. The pie was moving faster than expected. Free pie, it seemed, was not enough. People gladly paid for more, happy to get their second choice or even their third when their favorite disappeared, inhaled by another customer farther down the counter.

Perhaps little Mindy was right. Perhaps the pies *were* charmed. The pie eaters did indeed seem bewitched, transported to some preternaturally happy and serene place while eating, but looking anxious and agitated when the last crumbs disappeared from their plates, eyes darting to the pie case, hands raised to get Chloe's attention, as eager as a student who knows the answer to a complex problem, the need to be first paramount.

So it was not surprising that Charlie let out a little whoop when he saw Martha and Mindy pushing through the door, straining from the weight of their pie baskets.

"What'd I tell you?" Mindy said in greeting, looking at the empty pie case.

"Hope it's okay," Martha said. "Mindy was just dead set that you'd need more, so . . ."

"Oh, absolutely," Charlie said. "She's right. Your pie is truly magical."

Martha blushed. "Oh, go on. It's just pie."

"Well, not to all these people." Charlie nodded toward the customers at the counter, who were eyeing the baskets like owls would a plump mouse scurrying across the snow.

He grabbed a basket from each of them and motioned for them to follow him behind the counter, where they unloaded the pies into the pie case. As the clamor for "more pie" rose, he took both of them by the arm and walked them out to the parking lot. "I know it would be an extra burden," he said, "but could you possibly make *another* batch today?"

Martha smiled broadly at him. "Oh, no, that would be just fine with us, wouldn't it Mindy?"

Mindy nodded absently, distracted and visibly disturbed by the plume of smoke rising behind the diner.

Charlie turned and looked at the smoke. "Oh that, that's nothing, Mindy. Nothing to worry about."

"Maybe," she said. "Where there's smoke . . ."

Charlie let it go. "So . . . can I give you guys a ride home? It's pretty darn cold to be walking back and forth."

Martha shook her head. "No need. We like the walk and the cold don't bother us none. You go on back to the diner, and we'll see you later."

She grabbed Mindy by the hand and headed back toward the road, Mindy still looking over her shoulder at the smoke.

"Okay, then," Charlie called after them. "Be careful of those cars."

Martha turned and gave him a little smile. Charlie waved and then headed back toward the diner, once again focused on the smoke rising above the trees. *Must be Heph*, he thought. When he had a chance, maybe later, he'd have to have a talk with him about moving on. That, and call Larry again about the damn signs.

Right now, though, he had customers to tend. The breakfast crowd was beginning to thin, some rushing to their cars to make the most of Saturday, others reluctantly stepping outside, rubbing their newly rounded bellies, using toothpicks to probe for the last remaining morsels of a meal they'd tell their friends about, no doubt, while others lingered inside, content to blur the lines between breakfast and lunch, the siren call of the blue-plate special and free pie keeping them glued to their stools and embedded in their booths, nursing their third cup of Chloe's Joe and thinking life couldn't get much better than this.

Chloe came up behind Dee, who was staring out the window, watching Charlie escort Martha and Mindy into the parking lot.

"I think Martha is sweet on him," said Chloe.

Dee turned, startled. "Well, who wouldn't be? That's one handsome man."

"Listen to you, talkin' about a married man."

Dee smiled. "Oh, no, his wife died years ago."

Chloe gawked at Dee. "Dead? What happened?"

"Dunno, he's pretty quiet about it."

"But he's still wearing a ring."

"Hard to let her go, I think. I tried a couple of times to get him to talk about her, but he just clams up. Something terrible must have happened."

"Well, that explains another thing," said Chloe.

"What's that?"

"The way you've been staring at him, like you wanted to eat him with a spoon."

"Well, never you mind that. Anyway, I have some napkins to fold and you'd best tend to that guy at the end of the counter before he needs a drool bib."

CHAPTER 12

WHEN CHARLIE STEPPED BACK INSIDE, he spotted Dee and her daughter, Pearl, sitting in the corner booth, the one reserved for staff breaks and meals, the filling of salt and pepper shakers, and the making of silverware sets. Even from this distance, he could tell that the two were in mid-argument about something, both leaning forward across the table, noses nearly touching, the sound of their voices carrying above the noise of the diners, who were well aware of the heated battle, alternately glancing over at the pair and then turning away, shaking their heads, wondering when, if ever, it would just stop so they could eat in peace.

Charlie made his way quickly to the booth and slipped in beside Dee, startling both of them to silence. "Well, this must be Pearl," he said, smiling and offering his hand as if nothing was going on.

Pearl was her mother in miniature, just as beautiful, with the same penetrating golden eyes. Lighter of skin, more latte than cocoa, she seemed to be about the same age as Mindy and about as precocious. She greeted his outstretched hand with a look of disgust, as if he had offered her a dead fish, crossing her arms and slumping back in the booth, her eyes averted, her lower lip tucked under in full pout.

"Pearl, you sit up *right now* and say hello to Mr. Brace," Dee whispered harshly.

Charlie held up a hand. "No need," he said. "What seems to be the problem?"

Dee let out a heavy sigh. "Oh, she's just being stubborn—*again*—wants to play outside by herself."

Her comment made Pearl clench her arms tighter to her chest and glance quickly at Charlie.

"She's *mean*," Pearl said through clenched teeth.

"No, no," Charlie said. "She just knows about the *witch* who lives in the woods." He pointed out the window. "See, look over there at that smoke. It's from her fire. Must be cookin' up something . . . or *someone*."

Pearl turned her head and looked out the window. Smoke, gray and thick, was rising above the trees, and someone, a teenaged boy, was walking into the woods.

"Who's that?" she said, pointing.

Charlie looked out the window again, just in time to see Paulie disappearing into the woods, a cloth-draped plate of food in his hands. *What's up with that*? he thought

"Oh," Charlie said, thinking fast. "That's our Paulie, taking food to the witch so she won't eat any more of our customers."

Pearl's eyes widened as Dee did her best to look serious. *This Charlie Brace was something else*, Dee thought.

When he had slid into the booth, their thighs had briefly touched, Dee sliding away from him, not so fast that he'd be offended, but politely, to give him space. But the memory of the touch, the delicious shock of it, had had its effect on her, a big heat growing within. Now, as he talked to Pearl, leading her on about the witch, Dee stole glances at his face in profile, at his legs, his hands. *Oh, what hands he has!* she thought. *Those long fingers!* She breathed deeply, taking in his scent, parsing it out from the mélange of diner odors, like a hound searching for truffles.

She decided to take a chance, moving her leg against his. He flinched at first, then relaxed and pressed his leg back against hers. She leaned in a little more, letting her shoulder touch his, and he did not move away.

"Don't worry," Charlie continued, with a quick acknowledging glance at Dee. "I don't think she likes to eat little girls."

"You mean little *black* girls," Pearl shot back.

"Pearl, you *hush* now!" Dee snapped.

Charlie didn't skip a beat. "No, no, I mean she prefers little *boys*."

Pearl was quick to turn this to her advantage. "Then why can't I go outside and play?" She gave them both an arched-brow look that said *case closed, your honor*.

But her honor was having none of it. "Because the answer is *no*," Dee said.

Pearl slumped back in the booth again. "It's *always* no with you."

"Pearl!"

Charlie jumped in. "Wait, wait, I have an idea. Pearl, how would you like to play and earn some money, too?"

Pearl perked up. "Money?"

"Yeah, I need someone to add some numbers for me, so I can spend time with the customers. Are you good at numbers?"

Pearl beamed. "Mr. Brace, I am all about zero to nine. Teacher says I'm the *best* adder in class."

"Call me Charlie," he said. "Everybody does." He pressed his leg against Dee, the comment intended as much for her as for Pearl.

"Okay . . . Charlie," Pearl said. "How much?"

"Oh, it's about an hour's work . . ."

Pearl gave him an exasperated look. *"No,* I mean how much *money,* silly?"

Charlie pretended to ponder this, stroking his chin as if he had a beard. "Hmm, how about a dollar?"

Pearl frowned. "How about *two?"*

"Pearl!"

Charlie put his hand on Dee's forearm and let it linger there, Dee thrilling to his touch. "No, she's right. It's a big job—worth two dollars. Pearl, you've got yourself a deal."

Pearl clapped her hands together. "Two *dollars?* Wow! Bring on those numbers, Charlie."

"Okay, let me get them. And when you're done with the job, I have a surprise for you."

"Ooh, ooh, what is it?" Pearl said, bouncing in her seat, wide-eyed.

"Another little girl will be here, and if it's okay with your mom, the two of you can play out back a while."

Pearl turned to Dee, giving her an imploring look. "Please, mommy, *please*."

Dee smiled at her. "Well, if you do a good job . . ."

"I will! I will!"

"Then okay."

"Yes!" Pearl shouted, throwing her arms in the air.

Charlie laughed. "Well, I'm glad *that's* all decided."

He reluctantly moved his hand from Dee's arm and slid out of the booth. The longing look Dee gave him gave him goose bumps. And the look was not lost on Pearl, who glanced back and forth from one to the other, trying to figure out what these dreamy, goofy looks were all about. Had they both gone stupid or come down with a fever?

Pearl decided on stupid.

CHAPTER 13

JEANIE SAW THEM COMING BEFORE ANYONE ELSE, the mother and daughter trudging through the parking lot, burdened once more by pies, steam rising from their baskets, Martha's dress flapping wildly in the wind despite her best efforts to keep it under control with her free hand.

She tapped Chloe on the shoulder. "Look at 'em. How's that possible?"

Chloe stopped wiping the counter and glanced at the pair pushing through the door. "What do you mean? It's just Martha and Mindy."

"The pies, the *pies*. It's only been an hour. How could they possibly make one pie, let alone an entire batch?"

Chloe shrugged, not really interested. "Dunno. All I know is, I'm damn glad they're here."

"You got that right," Jeanie said. "Still . . ."

"Jeanie, give it a rest. I mean, it's not like the pies just materialized, like magic, out of thin air. They probably had them ready to shove into the oven, is all."

"I don't know. The way these customers gobble 'em down, you have to wonder. In fact, some of these customers are about as strange as the pies. The way they dress. How quiet they are. The way they avert their eyes when you try to strike up a conversation. And the way they eat those pies. I swear, it's like they're under some magic spell."

Chloe snorted. "Magic? Ha! That's a good one. Besides, if you want strange, there's always Paulie. That kid gives me the creeps."

"You got that right," Jeanie said, looking over at Paulie, who was at the opposite end of the diner, standing motionless, staring out the window, watching Martha and Mindy approaching the diner. Jeanie leaned in and whispered to Chloe. "Here we go again."

"Yeah, magic time," Chloe giggled, giving Jeanie a playful elbow poke before moving down the counter to refill a customer's mug.

"Well, *something* weird is going on here," Jeanie said under her breath, then turned to greet Martha and Mindy. "Boy, am I ever glad to see you two. We're nearly out."

Martha gave her a big smile, set her baskets on the counter, and then helped Mindy lift hers. "No problem," she said, looking around, trying not to meet the stares of the customers, who seemed to be as curious about the pie maker as they were eager to eat her wares. "Is Mr. Brace here?"

Jeanie glanced around, spotted him, and pointed him out. "There, in the back booth, with Dee's kid."

"Thanks." Martha turned to Mindy, who was staring intently at the booth and Pearl.

"Come on, Mindy, let's say hello to Mr. Brace."

Mindy just stood there. "But there's a little girl, momma."

"No matter, child." Martha grabbed her hand and tugged her forward, but Mindy resisted.

"But momma . . ."

"Mindy, you come now." She tugged harder, Mindy resisting at first but then relenting as they neared the booth.

Charlie saw them coming and slid over to make room, motioning Pearl to do the same. "Have a seat," he said, patting the bench.

Martha slid in next to Pearl.

"Sit next to Mr. Brace, Mindy."

Pearl, fresh from an error-free adding session, perked up. "Call him Charlie. *Everybody* does."

Martha turned and smiled at Pearl, then gave Mindy a menacing sit-down-now look, Mindy reluctantly sliding in next to Charlie, eyes averted, refusing to look at anyone.

"Charlie, can me and Mindy go play now," Pearl said, nodding toward Mindy, who looked up, alarmed.

"No way," she said firmly.

"Mindy, you listen," Martha said, leaning across the booth and putting her hand on Mindy's shoulder. "It will be okay."

"But momma . . ."

"No buts, baby, I have to talk to Mr. Brace here — *alone*. Now you run along and play with this nice little girl."

"Name's Pearl," Pearl said. "Like from the oyster."

"Yes," Martha said. "You go play with Pearl, now."

Mindy didn't budge.

"Mindy? You hear me?"

Mindy let out a big sigh. "Yes, momma." She slid out of the booth, as did Martha, making way for an eager, bubbly Pearl.

"Come on, Mindy," Pearl said. "Time's a wastin'." Pearl near pranced away, Mindy following slowly, reluctantly, looking back at her mother, giving her an imploring look.

"Scoot now." Martha said. "It'll be okay."

Pearl, then Mindy, pushed out the door and were gone, Martha staring intently at the door a few moments before turning back to Charlie, a look of deep concern on her face.

"Mr. Brace," she said, hesitating, searching for the right way to begin.

"Yes?"

"Mindy . . . and I, we . . . we're leaving town."

"What?" he said, much too loudly, every head in the diner turning to look at him. He held up a hand to indicate everything was okay, and mouthed *sorry* before turning back to Martha.

"What?" he whispered. He imagined his entire business crumbling like a pie crust.

"We *must* leave," she repeated.

"Must? But Why?"

Her lips began to quiver, tears coming to her eyes. "That man . . . in the woods . . . *scares* me."

Charlie reached across the table to touch her hand, but she pulled back, shaking her head.

"Don't, please," she said.

"I only meant—"

"To calm me, yes, I know that, but I'm not some silly woman, Mr. Brace. I'm not *paranoid*."

"No, of course not," Charlie said, pulling his hand back. "But really, I've talked to that old man, and he seems harmless enough."

"*Harmless?*" She spit out the word and gave Charlie a withering look. "I know this man—*know* him!"

"But—"

"What name is he using *this* time? Zeus? Pan? Hephaestus? It's always a god's name."

Charlie blinked at *Hephaestus*. "He used Hephaestus, I mean Heph, but he seemed so, so—"

"Well, he's *not*. He's pure *evil*, and he's been stalking me and my baby—won't leave us alone."

Charlie couldn't think what to say, and she could see the puzzled look on his face.

"It's about *revenge*, for a slight from my husband. A business deal gone bad."

"But surely he can't blame you."

Martha laughed sardonically. "Oh, Mr. Brace, please."

She leaned across the table, eyes fixed on his. "He put a curse on us, vowed to track us down—long as it took, he said—and so far, he's kept that promise."

"He's done this *before?*"

"Many times, from town to town to town." She slumped back in the booth. "It never ends."

"Have you told the police?"

"Worse than useless. Hands are tied, they say, until he actually hurts us—as if *hurt* can only be physical."

"So he hasn't touched you or Mindy?"

"No, not yet. He's just there, always there, on the edge of things, watching us, lurking, waiting for his chance."

"Look," Charlie said, "I don't want you to leave. Let me talk to him, send him on his way."

Martha seemed skeptical. "I'm not sure that'll do any good. As long as *we're* here, *he'll* be here."

"Don't be so sure, Martha. Just give me a chance. And if it doesn't work, I'll get the police to *arrest* him for trespass."

Martha brightened. "You'd do that?"

"Yes, of course. Listen, he likes to pick through my garbage every night. I'll talk to him and send him away—*tonight*—I promise."

"Oh, Mr. Brace, that would be *wonderful!*" She reached out and touched his arm.

"Wow, your hands are *cold*," he laughed, shattering the tension.

"Oops, sorry," she said, pulling back. "Cold hands, warm heart—or so I'm told."

"Must be from that long walk in the cold. You really should wear gloves."

"I guess."

He grew more serious. "Listen, will you be okay till tonight? You could stay here or back at my place."

She shook her head. "No, we'll be fine. We have ways to keep him out of the house, and he won't bother us along the road. I'm just afraid he'll come into the diner after us, like he did before."

"Before?"

"Yeah. Another time, a while back."

"So what happened? He didn't hurt you, did he?"

Tears welled in her eyes again. "I'd rather not . . ."

"Sure," Charlie said, "sure."

Martha looked up at him again. "You'll run him off, then?"

"Like I said, yes."

She turned away and wiped her tears. "Thank you."

CHAPTER 14

MINDY AND PEARL EXPLODED INTO THE DINER, Mindy bouncing and giggling, Pearl in tears, trembling, her dress torn at the shoulder and muddy.

Dee took one look at her, threw down the cloth she'd been using to clean the counter, and rushed to her side.

"Pearly, what happened?"

"Her," she sobbed, pointing at Mindy, who had retreated behind her mother's skirt. "She *attacked* me!"

"Did not," Mindy said, sticking her head out, and her tongue.

"Did too!"

"She fell."

"You pushed me!"

"Did not."

"Did too!"

"Did not!"

"Did—"

"Hush, both of you," Dee said, separating them and moving between them.

"Yes, you stop that right now," Martha said, pushing Mindy behind her and holding her there.

Dee grabbed Pearl by the shoulders, twisted her around, and pushed her in the direction of Charlie, who was staring drop-jawed at the scene.

"Pearl, you go sit in that booth with Charlie."

"Yes, ma'am," Pearl said, sniffling and walking away, her lips quivering, one hand to her shoulder to hold up her dress.

Dee watched her go, then turned back to Martha and glowered at her. "I don't know *what* happened out there, but I think it *best* that your little girl stay away from Pearl—*understand?*"

Martha returned ice for ice. "Yeah, I understand. Come on, Mindy, let's get out of this place. We have pies to bake." She grabbed Mindy by the arm and tugged her toward the door.

"But I didn't do *anything*, momma."

"Shush, girl, and come on." And then they were gone, the door clicking shut behind them.

Dee watched them go, both of them arguing and shouting at each other as they walked through the parking lot to the road. *Look how she sasses her mother*, Dee thought. *I wouldn't let Pearl do that.*

She turned away from the window and walked to the back booth, where Charlie had his arms around Pearl, holding her close and stroking her hair. *He is one good man*, Dee thought.

Charlie saw her coming and slid over to make room.

"Okay, Pearl," Dee said, sliding in next to Charlie, her leg pressing firmly against him. "What *happened* out there?"

Pearl sighed heavily. "She ripped my dress and pushed me into a puddle."

"And what did *you* do to deserve that?" Dee said.

Pearl looked down at her lap. "Nothin'."

"Nothin'?"

Pearl's lips began to tremble again. "I just saw . . ."

"Saw? Saw what?"

"What she did."

"Which was what?"

Pearl shook her head. "Nothin'."

"Oh, so you're back to *nothin'* again?"

"Yeah," Pearl said in a small voice.

"Pearl," Dee said, raising an eyebrow. "There must have been *something* you did or said. She seems so *nice.*"

Pearl looked up, incredulous, her eyes darting from her mother to Charlie and back again. "*Nice?* She's not nice. She's *mean*, and *weird*—all she talks about is pies and the smoke coming from the woods. Doesn't know anything about anything—not games, not songs, not presidents . . ."

"Pearl, how can you say such things about such a nice little girl like that?"

"Stop with the nice. Momma, I could see right through her! She's scary mean and—"

"Hush!"

"But she's not—"

Dee held up a finger, glaring at her to stop, Pearl slumping back in the booth, nearly in tears. "No one listens to me, *ever*, she sniffed, both of them becoming quiet.

Charlie took the opportunity to change the subject. "Oh, there's something you *both* don't know about the man in the woods."

Both of them turned to look at Charlie.

"He's apparently been stalking and harassing them."

"Wow, that's terrible," Dee said.

"Not what that Mindy said," Pearl said, crossing her arms smugly, waiting for them to pry the information from her.

Dee said nothing, just cocked her head to one side and launched a withering arched-brow look at her daughter. Pearl met the look with one of her own, the two of them locked in brow-to-brow combat.

Charlie intervened. "What do you mean, Mindy?"

"Okay," Pearl said. "You want weird, I'll give you weird. *Nice* little Mindy said the man in the woods is a demon straight from hell and that she was going to kill him with a poisoned pie."

Charlie and Dee laughed despite themselves.

"You see," Pearl said. "I laughed, too, and that's when she attacked me."

"Honey," Dee said, reaching across the table and stroking Pearl's hair. "She's just scared, is all."

"Yeah," Charlie said. "It's a defense mechanism, a way of dealing with her fears."

Pearl wasn't buying it. "Well, she didn't look afraid to me."

"Oh, honey," Dee said. "She's just a frightened little girl."

"More like frightening," Pearl shot back

"Okay, okay, enough of this," Dee said. "Let's get you home and cleaned up."

Pearl threw up her arms, exasperated.

Dee turned to Charlie. "Okay if I take a break, boss? Won't be more than half an hour."

Charlie nodded. "Sure thing. You two run along. The crowd has thinned a bit, so we'll be fine."

"Thanks," Dee said, smiling at him warmly, leaving little doubt about her feelings for him. Charlie returned the smile, his eyes locked on hers.

A blind man could see where they were headed, but Pearl was just plain puzzled by it all.

"Talk about weird," she mumbled.

CHAPTER 15

THE THIN CROWD FATTENED UP MINUTES AFTER Dee and Pearl had headed home, an all-Latino soccer team and their entourage tromping into the diner, raising the decibel level with laughs and shouts and victory whoops. Charlie worked the counter, filling in for Dee, and tried his best to protect Chloe from the sexual entreaties of the team, or at least two members of the team. While the rest of the team sat politely, if loudly, reviewing the menu and chatting with their friends about the winning goal, these two loudly praised Chloe's many physical charms and described in graphic detail what they would like to do if she would only give them the opportunity.

Chloe stood her ground as best she could, ignoring their comments and taking and serving orders as quickly and politely as possible. But Jesus, observing her plight from his position at the sandwich station, was having none of it. He selected his biggest knife and moved down the counter, twirling it in his hand like a baton, saying something firmly in Spanish—what, Charlie didn't know—but it quickly silenced them, each burying his head in a menu. Satisfied, Jesus returned to his sandwich station with Charlie in his wake.

"*That* was something," Charlie said. "What did you say to them?"

Jesus picked up a bread knife and began to work his magic on a chicken club sandwich. "I told them that my father was a pig farmer and had taught me many things about knives."

"I don't get it," Charlie said, puzzled.

Jesus made a quick motion in the air with his knife, and smiled. "Castracíon . . ."

"Oh," Charlie laughed, "oh, my."

"Yes, a *big* oh-my."

Charlie patted him on the back and headed back down the counter, winking at Chloe as he approached her.

She grabbed him by the arm. "What did Jesus say to them?"

Charlie leaned in and whispered in her ear.

"Whoa," she laughed, turning to look down the counter at Jesus, who gave her an acknowledging nod. "That's amazing, I've got to tell Jeanie."

She scooted down the length of the counter and whispered in Jeanie's ear. Jeanie slapped her thigh and let out a guffaw that would have outdone a jackass. "Hot damn," she said, "hot damn!"

From there, the translation went from Jeanie to Jimmy to Paulie to Monroe, who let out a laugh so infectious and booming that even the soccer players had to join in.

Dee, returning from home, looked from person to person, trying to figure out what the big joke was. Chloe spotted her and rushed up to fill her in.

"He said that?" Dee said. "Wow."

"You should have seen it. He was amazing."

"Sounds like." Dee waved at Jesus to get his attention and then gave him a big thumbs up, which he acknowledged with a wink and a shrug as if to say *no big deal, it was nothing.*

"We'd best get back to work," Dee said, taking in the size of the crowd. "These guys look hungry."

"You got *that* right, and they *pinch*," Chloe giggled.

"Not *my* ass, they don't. Come on, let's do it."

Thirty minutes later, their hunger sated, at least for food, the team quietly departed, leaving the diner half empty and its sinks half full.

Charlie was about to lend a hand washing dishes when he noticed Grace Sharp standing just inside the doorway, looking from side to side, taking in all that could be seen and smelled of a diner that had once been hers. She was dressed all in black, with tight-fitting slacks emphasizing her long legs, a turtleneck showing off her breasts but covering her neck to hide the most visible evidence of her age. If anything, though, she looked even more beautiful to Charlie than when they had first met. And despite his growing affection, maybe love, for Dee, he knew he was powerless to resist anything Grace might ask of him.

He and Dee reached her at the same time.

"One for lunch?" Dee said, motioning her toward an empty booth.

Before Grace had a chance to reply, Charlie swooped in, snatched the menu out of Dee's hand, and stepped between her and Grace.

"I'll take this one," he said, giving Grace a big smile, which she returned in full measure. "I was hoping you'd come."

He and Grace moved away to the booth, leaving Dee just standing there, fuming. *I was hoping that you'd come? she thought. What does that mean? Who is this woman? And why is she looking at Charlie like that? And just look at him, he's practically drooling!*

Miffed and more than a little jealous, she nevertheless gathered herself up and set about her work, putting two glasses of water on a tray, along with napkin-wrapped silverware, and heading for their booth.

"Have you decided?" she said coolly to Grace.

"Um," Grace said, opening the menu.

"I guess not," Dee said, setting the silverware and glasses down so hard that people turned their heads and water sloshed out of the glasses. Then, without so much as a glance at Charlie, she turned on her heels and flounced away, leaving Charlie stunned.

"What's with her?" Grace said.

Charlie shook his head. "She's been having a bad day."

"I guess, but talk about *rude.*"

Charlie quickly changed the subject. "So . . . what do you think of the diner?"

She smiled at him. "Honestly?" she said, looking around. "It gave me goose bumps. Everything is so familiar, and yet different. I love what you've done with the red leather. I must say, the smell of grease and new leather is downright *intoxicating.*"

Charlie laughed at this. "Well, it's actually fake leather, but . . ."

"Well, real or faux, Bill and I could never afford *that* upgrade. We were operating on a shoestring . . ."

She seemed to drift off, her face revealing a deep inner pain. Charlie attempted to bring her back.

"Oh, then you'll love this. I got all that leather installed for the cost of a blue-plate special on Saturday night."

Grace brightened. "We used to do the same thing, swapping food for services. Once—oh, you'll love this—once we actually swapped food for food.

"Food for food?"

"Yeah, a meal for a meal deal with the owner of a Chinese restaurant."

"Wow, I'll have to give that a shot—I love Chinese."

"Yeah, me too."

Charlie had a brief vision of the two of them at a Chinese restaurant. They would eat and laugh, and finally Charlie would reach out and touch her hand, his fingers and hers interlocking as they stared dreamily into each others eyes and leaned in for a kiss. Despite the age difference, there was no doubt that he was strongly attracted to her and under her spell.

Dee could see that attraction in his face—*and hers, the bitch*—when she returned with her order pad and pen poised in front of *her like a shield and a dagger.*

"*Ready now?*" she snapped.

Grace looked up at her in disbelief. How could Charlie put up with such a surly waitress?

"Yes," she said coolly. "I'll just have coffee, black, no cream."

"Joe, check, and you sir?" she said, quickly turning to Charlie, her lips tightly pursed.

Charlie ignored her. "Grace, how about some pie to go with that? We have *amazing* pie."

Grace glanced up at Dee. "If it's not too much *trouble,*" she said, her tone as saccharine as she could muster, "I'll have some apple pie."

"Not at all," Dee said, giving tone for tone and then clicking over to Charlie. "And you sir?" she said, leaving little doubt about her anger.

Charlie ignored the tone. He'd talk to her later. "The same," he said.

"Fine," Dee said, scribbling down the order.

"Fine," Charlie said.

Dee stormed away, Charlie and Grace shaking their heads, watching her go.

"Looks like you've got a problem there," Grace said. "If I were you . . ."

"No, she'll be okay. I'll talk to her later. It's not like her, really. Her daughter was attacked by another little girl about an hour or so ago. She's still upset, I guess."

"Attacked? How horrible."

"Oh, nothing *major*, really. Just kids being kids."

"Still . . ."

"Yeah . . . anyway, I've been meaning to ask, why did you change your mind about coming to the diner?"

She smiled at him warmly. "You made an *impression* on me, Charlie."

"An impression, what kind of impression?"

"Oh, a good one, as a man who could make a go of it. I guess I was just curious how it was turning out."

Charlie raised both arms and swept them in the air. "So, what do you think?"

She didn't look around, just looked deeply into his eyes. "I think I *like* what I see."

Charlie could feel himself blushing. "Um, well thank you," he stammered.

Grace threw back her head and laughed. "Oh, Charlie, you're blushing. I meant the *diner*."

"Oh," Charlie said, feeling the blush deepening. "Oh, of course, I knew that."

"Not that I don't find you *attractive*," she said, giving him that seductive look again. "I do."

Dee saved Charlie from further embarrassment by returning with the coffee and pie, which she set before them with a faux flourish of exaggerated politeness, as if she were serving pheasants to a king and his queen.

"Two Eves, two Joes," she said. "Will there be anything else?"

Charlie and Grace looked up at her and shook their heads.

"No," Grace said, "this will be fine."

"Very well," Dee said. "Enjoy." And with that she was gone, leaving Grace amused.

"She is *too much*."

"Yeah," Charlie said. "She is that. So . . . try the pie. We have it delivered fresh several times a day. People are crazy about it."

Grace first took a sip of her coffee. "Mmm, the coffee is perfect."

"Thanks to you."

"You're quite welcome, sir," she laughed. "And now to this pie. It looks great."

She cut a small piece with her fork and took a tentative bite. Her expression changed from playful to alarmed in an instant. She blanched, went wide-eyed, and dropped the fork.

"Who *made* this?" she barked, looking quickly around, a look of horror on her face.

Charlie, stunned, began to speak but Grace stopped him. "Don't tell me—a woman and a little girl who just showed up one day with pies—am I right?"

"Yes, but—"

"I've got to get out of here," she said, grabbing her purse and heading for the door faster than Charlie could keep up with her.

"Grace, *wait*, I—"

When she reached the door, she turned and snapped at him. "Didn't you look at what my lawyer gave you?"

"Yes, I *did*," Charlie said, equally puzzled and alarmed. "Why, what's wrong?"

"You're in danger, Charlie. Look at the folder, it's *all* there."

"All of what? What do you mean?"

"Not now, you wouldn't believe me, anyway. Just look at the damned folder and give me a call."

"But—"

"Sorry, I've got to get out of here." She turned away from him, walked quickly out of the diner, and drove away in her pink Cadillac, spraying gravel as she sped across the parking lot to the road, where the tires gained purchase with a squeal as the rubber met the road and the car lurched into traffic.

"What the—" Charlie stood there, watching the car accelerate and disappear.

CHAPTER 16

CHARLIE'S FIRST IMPULSE WAS TO RUSH BACK to his apartment and look at the folder again. How could he have possibly missed something that would put him in danger? And why was Grace so upset about Martha and Mindy? But the second, overpowering impulse was to stay put. He was not about to abandon his diner. Whatever danger awaited would have to be sorted out later, when the crowd thinned to late-night coffee drinkers, insomniacs, and couples in the throes of love, reluctant to call it a night.

Besides, he had to have a word with Larry, who was having pie and coffee at the counter, waiting to fill him in on this latest attempts to fix the signs.

Charlie got right to the point. "Did you fix 'em?"

Larry took another sip of coffee, set down his cup, and swallowed. "Nothin' *to* fix. I've checked the circuits, did some jumper tests to try and isolate the problem, even tested the transformers, and I can't find a damn thing wrong."

"But the signs are still buzzing and flickering," Charlie said, perhaps too angrily.

"Now, now, don't go getting' your shorts in a twist. I know they're still flickering to beat the band."

"Then what do you intend to do about it?"

"I know this guy in Baltimore, a real journeyman electrician who knows neon so well he's known as Neon Bob."

"Neon Bob?" said Charlie, incredulous.

"Yeah, I've asked him to take a look. He said fine, he loves a challenge, and it's not going to cost you extra."

"All right, when's he coming? It can't be too soon."

"Probably tomorrow or the next day," said Larry, standing up and tossing some spare change on the counter, his idea of a generous tip. "As soon as he can fit us in."

And with that, Larry tipped his hat and strode from the diner.

Two hours later, at 5:00 p.m., the dinner crowd arrived, seemingly on cue, and kept coming until well past 8:00 p.m. Unlike the lunch crowd, which was vocal and boisterous, the dinner crowd was quiet and subdued, the tinkle of silverware and the soft murmur of quiet conversations the dominant sounds.

His staff, fatigued from wave after wave of customers, seemed to heave a collective sigh of relief from this new, relaxed pace, and took time to pause and joke around with each other.

All but Dee, that is. She was still in a deep funk about Grace and how Charlie had looked at her. She thought Chloe would be her stiffest competition for Charlie because she was white, beautiful, and better endowed. But his obvious attraction to Grace, who was much older, baffled her, making her wonder if he harbored some as-yet-undisplayed racial prejudice. Maybe he didn't love her, or even *like* her, after all. She tried to shake off that thought. Then she thought he might be acting this way because she was married, at least technically. Charlie had never given her reason to doubt his affection or sincerity. Still, the thought lingered and festered, her mind leapfrogging logic to roll film of Charlie fucking Grace, on the counter, in the parking lot, in the backseat of that damned pink Cadillac of hers.

Charlie, taking note of her mood, gave her wide berth throughout the evening, smiling perhaps too broadly at her when they passed but not stopping to talk. He would talk to her later, when she had calmed down, *if* she had calmed down. Right now, though, he had to fulfill his promise to Martha, and talk to Hephaestus.

Paulie, returning from a trip to the dumpster, had told him Hephaestus was out there, digging through the trash. So he had taken off his dishwashing apron and stepped out into the night, which was clear and starry and cold, his breath coming in white puffs.

The sounds coming from the dumpster sounded more like a foraging bear than an old man.

"Hephaestus?" he said loudly. "Is that you?"

The sounds stopped immediately.

"Heph?" he repeated.

"Yeah, it's me," Hephaestus said, stepping out of the dumpster with a half-filled sack. "You were maybe expecting the president?"

Charlie got right to the point. "We need to talk."

"About the moon? Just look at her." He turned away from Charlie and pointed up at the moon. "I love her when she's like this, when you can't tell whether she's waxin' or wanin'. That's when she's most like a woman, don't you think?"

"What?" Charlie said, confused.

"Too deep for you, eh?"

"Look, I—"

"No matter. Let's keep it simple. Kind of looks like someone took a bite out of her, a little nibble, don't it?"

"Yeah, well . . ."

"Or more like a Cheshire Cat's smile, maybe?"

"Listen, no, I'm not here to talk about the moon."

Hephaestus chuckled and held open his sack for Charlie to see what was inside. "Then it must be about these sorry French fries. Dumpster's full of them. Your oil is all wrong. What you need to do is—"

"Whoa, stop," Charlie said with growing impatience. "It's not about the damned French fries; it's about *you*."

"*Me?*" Hephaestus gave him a look that said *you've got to be kidding.*

"Yeah, you. People have been complaining about you, so I want you to move on."

Hephaestus looked left, right, and all around. "What *people?* There's only us. No one else has seen me. Okay, maybe one of your busboys. Is that who complained, that kid?"

"No," Charlie said, "others have seen you and are frightened by you."

Hephaestus looked startled. "*Frightened?* Look at me, am I frightening?"

"What *I* think isn't important. I have to do what's right for my customers."

Hephaestus snorted. "Is picking on a helpless old man down on his luck *right?*

Charlie had had enough. "Look," he said sternly, "this is *my* property and I want you off of it—*now*—or I'll call the cops."

Hephaestus let his arms drop to his sides. "So that's the way it's going to be?"

"Yes, that's how it's *got* to be."

Hephaestus sighed, threw his sack over his shoulder, and bowed. "As you wish, sir."

He turned and walked away, looking up at the moon as he went. "Some see a waxin' moon and swear that it's wanin', some see a sunny day and swear that it's rainin'."

He stopped and turned back to Charlie. "I wonder what *you* see, Mr. Brace. I mean really *see*."

Charlie did not respond, but stood his ground.

"Humph. Sometimes it's not about seeing one thing or another, you know, but about seeing *anything at all*. Don't choose to be blind. There's no hope for you then, son."

He turned away again, walked into the woods, and disappeared into the waxing darkness.

CHAPTER 17

As MIDNIGHT APPROACHED, Charlie turned the diner over to a surprised Jesus, who readily agreed to stay on beyond his shift to give Charlie a break, raising his arms in the air, giving a little shout, and making a pointed remark to Monroe. "Guess who's in charge now, big fella!"

Monroe turned away and raised his eyes to the ceiling. "God, help us."

Minutes later, Charlie was back in his apartment, which seemed like an alien landscape to him. Everything was just as he had left it when he had rushed out to get to the diner before sunrise, but somehow, the day had changed him, or at least the way he viewed himself and his pre-diner life. The furniture, the magazines, the pictures on the wall, all seemed to belong to someone else, except perhaps for the framed photograph of Lara, smiling up at him from the desk. Each time he looked at it, her smile seemed to change.

The folder was on the kitchen table where he'd left it. He cleared away a dish containing the uneaten crusts of an industrial-grade frozen pizza, the remains of a late-night snack he'd eaten days before, and took it to the sink. The crusts were now as hard as bone.

He went back to the table. What could Grace be talking about? What had he missed?

After briefly glancing at the Bramson Diner brochure and tossing it aside, he sorted the contents of the folder into three piles: legal papers, correspondence, and news clippings and photographs.

The legal papers were just that, a sea of whereases, official seals, and parties of the first and second parts. He pushed those aside. The correspondence between owners and buyers was equally uninteresting, offering little more than a lesson in tone, the owners hawking the diner and the joys of ownership, the buyers feigning disinterest in an attempt to reduce the price and hide their still-obvious zeal to buy.

Finally, he was down to the news clippings and the old photograph of Becky Swanson serving up a slice of pie to a barefoot little girl in overalls. He picked it up and studied it. Becky stared out at him as dour as can be, the little girl sitting there, her back turned to Charlie, hands reaching up to take the plate. He set the photo aside and turned to the clippings.

The first showed Tom Davis standing outside the brand-new diner with his staff—*nothing*. Charlie scanned it again, looking at every person—*still nothing*. He tossed it aside.

The second showed Bill and Grace Sharp serving up food to a customer—*again nothing*. Still, Charlie lingered on this clipping. Grace was so beautiful and seemingly happy and carefree. The death of her husband had certainly changed her, perhaps more than the passing years, and he could probably say the same thing for himself.

The third clipping was Bill and his little league team—*no*. The fourth, the clipping about Bill's death—*maybe*. He had died shouting about something, or maybe *at* someone. Grace had been tight-lipped about his death, and Charlie didn't want to intrude on her grief. Even after this many years, it would be unseemly. But was her demeanor about grief or something else?

Finally, he picked up the clipping of Grace and Bill serving up food to the poor, who were lined up outside the diner soup-kitchen style. He noticed the R in the DINER sign was out.

Damn!

He scanned the photo again, going from face to down-trodden face, abruptly stopping on a bearded man near the end of the line. He was wearing what appeared to be a checkered tablecloth over his shoulders.

Heph!

Charlie felt a chill and a shock go through him. Heph looked *exactly* the same. Charlie checked the date on the clipping. *Jesus*, he thought, *this was taken seven years ago, but he hasn't changed a bit.* He tried to rationalize this in his own mind, knowing that some people never seem to age. His own father had looked years younger than his age, right up until his death. Still, the picture of Heph was spooky.

He was about to put the clipping down when he noticed two other figures in the line. Martha and

Mindy stared out at him, looking exactly, *impossibly* the same as they did now. Each carried a basket at their sides. They weren't there to receive food, but to *deliver* it.

Something else: Mindy was barefoot and wearing overalls. He dropped the clipping and grabbed the photograph of Becky Swanson. The little girl was Mindy! And this photo was taken over *twelve* years ago.

Charlie sat there a moment, stunned, goose bump climbing upon goose bump, then pulled out his cell phone and punched in Grace's number.

The phone rang four times, then clicked over to Grace's voice, a recorded message that was preternaturally cheerful. "This is Grace Sharp. Sorry I missed your call. Please leave a message."

Charlie was about to do just that, but another thought came into his head: *What had Pearl said about Mindy?*

"Momma, I can see right through her."

His goose bumps became moose bumps. He clicked the phone shut, grabbed the clippings and the photo, and ran from the apartment.

CHAPTER 18

CHLOE SAW HIM FIRST, HIS WILD-EYED LOOK as he burst into the diner, searching frantically for something or someone, then settling on Dee, who had her back to him, serving up coffee to some jock from the college and his date, a buxom blonde with *cheerleader* written all over her.

Chloe moved quickly down the counter, tapped Dee on the shoulder, and motioned with her eyes for her to turn around. Dee, reacting to Chloe's alarmed look, glanced over her shoulder, then did a double-take. Charlie was walking quickly toward her, his expression a mix of urgency and concern. Every jealous thought evaporated as quickly as he approached. She could see in his eyes that whatever was wrong, he was coming to her, and her alone.

"What's wrong?" she said.

"Come with me, *now*," he said, perhaps louder than he had intended. He took her hand and pulled her toward the door.

"Wait, my customers—"

"Chloe can handle them—right Chloe?"

Chloe nodded and grabbed the coffee pot from Dee's hands. "Here, you won't be needing that." And then they were gone. Chloe watched them jump into Charlie's car and speed away before turning back to her customers, who like her, were perplexed by what they had just seen.

"What was *that* all about?" the jock asked.

"Beats me," Chloe replied absently. "Beats me."

Charlie waited until they were on the highway to say anything. "Sorry about that, but I needed to talk to you, alone."

"That's okay. Is it about that woman?"

"What?" he said, confused. Then he realized she was talking about Grace. "No, of course not."

"Oh, well, I just thought—"

"No, it's about Pearl. I need to talk to her."

This completely threw Dee. "Pearl? But why?"

"Something she said about Mindy."

"Huh?"

"I didn't put it together right away, but then it just clicked, what she said."

Dee shook her head. "What clicked? Charlie, what the *hell* are you talkin' about?"

Charlie looked over at her and attempted a smile. "Sorry, I guess I'm babbling."

"You think?"

"Okay," he said, taking a deep breath. "Let me start over. Remember, earlier today, when Pearl said she could see right through Mindy?"

"Yeah, that she was mean, not nice."

"No, I think she could actually *see* right through her."

Dee laughed. "You're pulling my leg, right? You're not saying my baby sees dead people, are you?"

"Maybe. Look, I know it sounds crazy—"

"*Crazy* doesn't quite capture it, Charlie. Don't go all *Sixth Sense* on me. Seeing right through someone is just an expression, and that's all."

"I don't think so, not this time."

"What, you're saying that Mindy is a . . . *ghost?* Don't you think my baby would have, oh, *mentioned* that to her mother?"

"Maybe she was afraid."

She began to laugh again. *He can't be serious*. But then he gave her a look that sent chills up her spine. "You're serious about this, aren't you?"

"Dead serious, and I have proof."

"Yeah? Like what?"

"Some old newspaper clippings and a photo."

"Show me."

Charlie realized he'd put the clippings and photo in his back pocket. "When we get there. I'm sitting on them."

"Okay, but are you sure we need to do this now? I mean, Pearl's asleep. Can't this wait till morning?"

Charlie looked over at her. "If I'm right, this can't wait another minute."

They grew silent, each staring through the windshield, watching the road disappear beneath them, a Cheshire Cat of a moon staring down at them as it arced across the sky toward morning.

CHAPTER 19

DEE SAT THERE, LOOKING BACK AND FORTH at the clippings, not believing what she was seeing, then shuddered and turned to Charlie, who had been watching her intently. Her eyes were tearing. "How is this *possible?*" she said. "And I let my baby *play* with her . . ."

"You didn't know," Charlie said, rubbing her shoulder. They were still sitting in the car, the engine still rumbling.

"But what *do* we know? I mean, *why* are they here and *what* do they want?"

"I don't know. What I *do* know is that Martha and Mindy don't like Heph, and that Grace and maybe Pearl know more than we do."

"And what does *Grace* say?" She didn't like saying her name.

"Nothing, at least not yet. I tried to call her but she wasn't in, or wasn't picking up."

He turned off the engine. "Come on, let's go talk to Pearl."

They climbed out of the car, Dee fumbling for her house keys. "Where the hell? Ah, here they are." She held up the keys, jingling them. "I think I spend half my life looking for my keys."

"I know what you mean. Every key should come with some kind of beeper that activates whenever you're more than ten feet away from it."

Dee laughed. "Well, I'd *definitely* buy that.

"Then I'll just have to invent it."

You do that. Okay, come on, let's get inside."

The small house, an old, one-floor clapboard, looking worn and tired and in desperate need of paint, was set back from the road, a stand of swaying white pines shielding it from the headlights of passing cars. It had clearly seen better days, but Charlie was not about to comment on its condition. He knew Dee was having a hard time making ends meet.

"Not much of a house," Dee said, "but Pearl and I like it."

"Don't apologize. Remember, I live above a liquor store. This looks like a palace."

"Yeah, well, it's pretty much a mess inside. Wasn't expecting company."

She turned the key in the lock and put her shoulder to the door, forcing it open. "Sticks a little."

Charlie ran his hand along the edge of the door. "I can fix that. Plane down the edge here, where it's sticking."

Dee smiled up at him. "Well, aren't you the handyman."

Charlie laughed. "Not really, but I inherited my dad's tools, so . . ."

"Okay," she said, "that would be nice."

She walked into the living room, threw her keys on the coffee table, and began picking up clothes from the floor and the couch. "You see, a complete mess."

"Well, by *my* standards, this is neat and tidy."

She stopped picking up clothes and threw the bundle she had onto a nearby chair. "Well, welcome to the palace—such as it is—let's go talk to the princess who lives here."

Charlie followed her down the hall and into Pearl's bedroom. Although Pearl was in bed, she was anything but asleep. Every light in the room was on, and all the shades had been pulled down to their maximum length, blocking the view of anyone or, to a child's mind, any *thing* that might be lurking outside.

Pearl, wide-eyed and startled by Charlie and her mother, took a tighter grip on her teddy bear.

"Hey, baby, it's just us," Dee said, sitting down on the edge of the bed and stroking Pearl's hair. "What's wrong?"

Pearl shook her head nervously. "Nothin', momma, just can't sleep." She looked up at Charlie. "Hi, Charlie, what're you doin' here?"

Charlie, who had been standing in the doorway, came over to the bed and sat next to Dee, taking care not to sit too close. "It's about Mindy."

Pearl cringed and pulled her covers up to her chin. Her lips were trembling.

"Baby, what is it?" Dee said.

"Let me guess," Charlie said. "Today's fight with Mindy wasn't just any fight. You could see right through her, couldn't you, just like she was—"

"A ghost!" Pearl blurted out. "She's a ghost for sure—and mean! One minute she was whole as you and me, momma, and then I startled her and she . . . *flickered!*"

Dee wrapped her arms around her. "Oh, baby, why didn't you tell me?"

"She said she'd kill me, momma—and *you*—if I said a single word to anyone." She looked over at Charlie. "You said it, not me, right? So it's okay . . ."

"Yes, of course," Charlie said, nodding. "You're totally in the clear."

"Whew," Pearl said, relieved. But then she frowned. "But *you're* not in the clear."

"What?" Charlie said.

"Mindy said, mostly, they want to kill *you*."

"Me? But why?"

"Dunno. Mostly she talked about that old man in the woods, what's his name."

"Hephaestus?" Charlie offered.

"Yeah, him," Pearl said. "She said he'd been chasing them down, but they were too tricky for him, and that soon they'd be rid of him forever."

"Kill him?" Dee said.

"Yeah, momma, I guess. She kept going on and on about poison pies, so maybe that's their plan."

"Well, don't you worry," Charlie said. "Your mom and I will figure out a way to stop them."

Pearl beamed. "Like Ghostbusters?"

"Yeah," Charlie laughed, "like Ghostbusters."

"Can I help?" Pearl asked, throwing back her covers.

"Whoa, whoa, baby," Dee said, pushing Pearl gently back down and tucking her in. "Of course you can help, but first all us Ghostbusters need to get some sleep."

"Oh, all right," Pearl said, pouting. Then she looked mischievously up at her mom. "If Charlie stays."

"Oh, you," Dee said, reaching down and tickling her.

"Stop, momma, stop!" she giggled.

"Okay, well maybe I can persuade Mr. Brace to stay for coffee. Now you get some sleep."

"How's that, Charlie?" Pearl said.

"Coffee sounds fine. I'll stay awhile. Now you get some sleep, princess."

"Okay, Charlie." She turned on her side, snuggling with her teddy, and closed her eyes.

Dee smiled at Charlie, put a finger to her lips, and began turning off lights.

Pearl, lying in the darkness now, cracked an eye and watched them tiptoe out of the room. *He called me princess!*

CHAPTER 20

DEE SHOOK HER HEAD, something she had been doing almost nonstop while Charlie recounted the history of the diner, from the day it rolled off the factory floor to the day Martha and Mindy walked through the door with what she now referred to as "those damn pies."

They were sitting on the couch, Charlie at one end, Dee at the other, her legs drawn up, knees to chin.

"Three things strike me as odd," she said finally. "I mean, apart from those damn flickering signs. *One*, why would that first owner have a custom wall put in at one end of the diner?"

Charlie shrugged. "Dunno, but custom work is fairly common"

"Still, I think it's odd. Anyway, *two*, what or who really killed Grace's husband? And *three*—and I know you'll think I'm crazy—what makes those pies so special? I mean, have you *seen* the looks on our customers' faces? It's like they've been transported to some special place, like they've been drugged."

It was Charlie's turn to shake his head. "I don't know about the pies, but Grace may be able to shed some light on the rest."

Dee glanced at her watch. "Shit, but *not* at 2:00 a.m. Too late to call."

Charlie glanced at his watch, too. "Wow, is it that late? I guess I should be heading back to the diner, check in on Jesus."

"Or you could stay," Dee said softly, sliding closer to him.

"Um . . ."

She was beside him now, her hands sliding behind his neck, drawing him to her.

CHAPTER 21

In his dream, he was sitting on a stool in his diner, flanked on either side by Martha and Mindy, Heph behind the counter, an idiotic grin on his face.

"The question is," he chuckled, "are they there or not?"

Charlie looked left and right. Martha scowled at him, and Mindy did the same. "There," he said.

Heph laughed and slapped the counter. "Look again, my friend."

Charlie looked left and right again. Martha and Mindy were gone, replaced on their stools by slices of pie. "Not there," he said, "but—"

"You just don't get it, do you?" Heph said, shaking his head. "Look again."

Charlie looked: Grace sat to his left, her eyes fixed on him, seductive; Dee sat to his right, her eyes loving moons.

"I don't get it," he said. "Grace and Dee are as real as you."

"Oh, really?" Heph said. "Dare I say it . . . look again."

Lara sat to his left and right and stood behind the counter, all three of her laughing louder and louder.

Charlie screamed and sat bolt upright in bed, the room, bathed in light by the rising sun, unfamiliar to him. In the time it took to mumble "where am I?" Dee had her arms around him.

"It's okay," she said, kissing him again and again on his neck. "You're in heaven."

"What?"

Dee laughed. "Well, that's what you told me last night."

He was fully awake now, the memory of last night's love-making overwhelming. He leaned in and kissed her softly. "And I'm still in heaven."

"So what's with the scream? A nightmare?"

"I screamed?"

"Big time."

"Well, it was a nightmare, all right. About Martha and Mindy. And Heph was in it, and so were you and Grace . . . and Lara, my wife."

"Lara?"

"Yes, she's in every dream of mine, it seems.

"But a nightmare?"

"Especially nightmares."

"You'll have to tell me more about that, Charlie."

"Yeah, sometime."

"No time like the present, or so they say."

Charlie heaved a heavy sigh.

"Or not," said Dee, screwing up her face into a mock pout.

"Don't do that," said Charlie. "I'll tell you about her—and her ghost."

"You *see* her?"

"Yeah, sometimes."

As eager as she was to talk about Lara and her ghost, she could see that Charlie wasn't ready to talk. She picked up his hand and placed it on her thigh. "So, do I feel like a ghost? Huh, do I?"

Charlie smiled and let his hand slide along her thigh, across her hip and up her back. "No, you feel—and look—*amazing*."

She pushed his hand away and sat Indian style, facing him. "So, what are we going to do about those *other* ghosts?"

"Well, I think the first thing we have to do is get dressed."

"No, seriously . . ."

Charlie sighed. "I think the first thing we do is talk to Grace. Not on the phone, though. In person. I want to see her face when we ask our questions."

Dee nodded, then frowned. "But what about the diner?"

"Yikes!" Charlie said. "We'd better get over there, pronto. Jesus is going to be hopping mad. I told him I'd only be gone an hour or so." He looked around frantically. "Where are my clothes?"

Dee raised an arm and pointed toward the door. "Scattered from here to the living room, like bread crumbs."

CHAPTER 22

JESUS WAS NOT ANGRY. He was livid. And like many people in such a state, he said more with his stiff posture and steely, narrow-eyed stare than he did with the words he forced through clenched teeth.

"I am an *artist*, not a manager, Mr. Brace. You had no call—*no call*—to leave me here with . . . with . . . all *this!*"

All this was a diner packed with entrenched, early-rising heathens and an army of just-released Sunday worshipers queued up at the hostess stand and out the door, all looking as if their prayers had inexplicably gone unanswered.

Charlie was about to say *I'm sorry*, but instead sighed heavily and said, "You're right, Jesus. I had no call. But from what I see here, you're an artist *and* a manager."

Jesus looked around quickly. Yes, the diner was full, but orders were being taken, food was being served and tables cleared with an efficiency approaching perfection, all to the tune of Monroe Brown's booming laugh and a counterpoint sizzle, like a violin's answer to a bassoon, coming from the grill.

Jesus shrugged and smiled. "I did my best."

"I can see that." Charlie paused, not quite sure how to put what he had to say next. "Um, look," he said, finally, "I know you're tired, but I need to ask a *big* favor."

Jesus, already shaking his head with disbelief, sensed what was coming next. "You've got to be kidding me . . ."

"Just an hour, Jesus, is all I need, not a minute more."

Jesus rolled his eyes to the ceiling. "But I've been here *twenty-four* hours."

"I know, I know," Charlie said, raising his hands in front of him, half expecting Jesus to charge. "And you can take off just as soon as I get back."

Jesus considered this. *"One hour, no more?"*

"Promise."

Jesus sighed heavily, his shoulders drooping. "Okay, you'll probably have to scrape me off the floor in an hour, but okay, go."

Charlie smiled and gave him a friendly slap on the shoulder. "Thank you!"

"Yeah, yeah," Jesus said, turning away. "Just go."

As Charlie left, he could hear Monroe's voice, an octave higher than usual, obviously taunting Jesus.

"Well, look who's in charge now."

He knew Jesus would fight back, but the door clicked behind him before he could hear the response.

A nervous, impatient Dee was waiting for him in the car. "Let's go!"

Charlie jumped into the car, and they sped away.

"How far is it?" Dee said after they had turned onto the interstate and settled comfortably into the middle lane.

"Surprisingly close, maybe ten minutes."

"You'd better call her, make sure she's there."

Charlie checked his watch. "She's probably still asleep."

"Maybe not," Dee said. "I hear *older* people rise earlier."

Charlie laughed. "What *is* it with you about Grace?"

Dee didn't hold back. "I don't like the way you *look* at her."

This puzzled Charlie. "*Really?* How exactly do I look at her?"

"You really want to know?"

"Yeah . . . how?"

She twisted around in her seat so she could watch his reaction. "Like you could *eat . . . her . . . up.*"

Charlie snorted. "But she's an *older* woman . . ."

"Eyes don't lie, Charlie. Admit it, you're attracted to her."

Yes, definitely, he thought. "Yeah, I guess I am, but *not* the way I'm attracted to you. Now *you*, you I could eat up."

Dee chuckled. "As I recall, you already did."

Charlie looked over at her lovingly. "Believe me, I wouldn't trade heaven for Grace."

Dee's mouth dropped open and then she began giggling.

"What?" Charlie said, smiling. How could anyone *not* smile when another person was giggling her head off. "What's so funny?"

"*Heaven* for *grace?*" Dee blurted out between giggles. "*Trade* heaven for *little-g* grace?"

"Oh," he said. "Didn't think."

"Yeah, anyway," Dee said, her giggles subsiding, "call her. If she's asleep, she'll need time to get dressed."

"Why would I want her to be dressed?" Charlie said, teasing.

Dee leaned over and punched him, hard, on the shoulder.

"Ouch!"

"Don't *mess* with heaven," Dee teased back.

He didn't, picking up his cell phone and punching in Grace's number with his thumb, laying further credence to the theory that the opposable thumb coupled with a cell phone separated humankind from all other species, for better or worse.

Grace did sound sleepy when she picked up, but when Charlie tried to apologize for waking her, she quickly interrupted him.

"Been up for hours, Charlie," she said, her voice a playful lilt. "Benefit of aging, like god wants to make it up to me for all the sunrises I missed in my somewhat wanton youth."

She paused, hoping to get a reaction out of him, but he was not about to play along, not with Dee at his side, straining to hear every word. All he could think to say was, "Good . . . I was worried I might wake you."

"No, not hardly. So . . . what's *up*, Charlie?"

He ignored the very clear sexual message, and got right to the point. "I need to talk to you . . . about the ghosts."

She paused. "So . . . you figured it out." Her voice was serious now.

"Not all of it, but some."

"You want to come over? I can fill you in, at least as much as I can."

"Yes, actually, I'm almost at your front door. Be there in about five."

"Okay, then," Grace said, but she was thinking *yikes!* As soon as she hung up, she raced to her bedroom closet and started looking for just the right slacks and that sexy new blouse, the one that accentuated her breasts.

CHAPTER 23

"She says it's okay," Charlie said, glancing at his watch. "Should be there in a few minutes."

"Okay," Dee said. "Charlie?"

"Yeah?"

"Have you ever seen a ghost before—I mean, before this?"

The memory clicked into place and played like a record in a jukebox. "In the first few days after Lara's death, I thought I saw her, but I can't be sure. It happened so fast. She was there, walking down the hallway one second, and gone the next. Maybe I just wanted to see her."

Dee saw how much this affected him, and tried to pull him in another direction. "Seen any other ghosts?"

"Seen? No, but I've heard them."

"Tell me."

Charlie told her. He had been in the basement of his house, fixing a flat on his bicycle, when he heard what sounded like a child running down the stairs from the second floor to the first and racing through the foyer, through the living room, and into the kitchen.

"Maybe some kid from the neighborhood?" Dee interrupted.

If only, Charlie thought. He had raced up the basement steps and searched the house, but found no one. "No," Charlie said, "every door and window was locked. I hate to admit it, but I'm a bit of a security freak, so there was no way I'd left anything unlocked."

Dee wondered where that need for security originated but let it go. "Interesting . . . but not very spooky."

"Well, it is when you consider that the previous owner of the house was born in the house . . . and died there."

"Ooh, it gets better. So you think the ghost-child was—"

"Dunno, but there's more. When her husband—this really old guy with the worst breath you can possibly imagine—was talking us up about buying the house, he said we could keep anything and everything in the attic we wanted."

"You and Lara?"

"Yes. Anyway, we thought the guy was nuts. The attic was filled with antiques: Civil War diaries, oil paintings, photos of dirigibles on glass plates, photo albums showing people in turn-of-the-century dress, a Rolls Royce shaving kit, even an Atwater-Kent radio—amazing stuff."

"Wow," Dee said, not knowing what an Atwater-Kent radio might be or why Rolls Royce would ever make a shaving kit, but impressed by Charlie's assessment of their value. "But what does this have to do with ghosts?"

"Let me back up a bit. When he told us about the stuff in the attic, he said there was no way he would go up there. At the time, we thought he meant he was too frail to go up there. He was really old, and the steps to the attic were narrow and steep. But that wasn't it at all."

"No?"

"No, we found out why he wouldn't go up there our first night in the house. We were just settling into bed when I heard a sound coming from the hallway."

"Wait, what did Lara wear to bed?"

"Huh?"

"Pajamas, a sexy negligee, *nothing?*"

"Um, well, those cotton pullover thingies."

"Nightgowns."

"Yeah, I guess, why?"

"Nothing. Go on."

Charlie tried to find his place in the story. "So . . . I heard this sound, kind of a rattling noise, so I went to the bedroom door and peered down the hall in the direction of the sound. The doorknob on the door to the attic was jiggling violently, like someone on the other side was trying to get out."

"Whoa, that's creepy!" Dee said, clutching herself, shivering. "Look at these goose bumps."

"And then, as if whatever or whoever was behind that door *knew* I was there, the jiggling just stopped."

"Wow, now *that's* a spooky story."

Charlie nodded. "Yeah, but there's more. The rest of the night, as we lay there, bug-eyed in bed, we could hear the sound of someone pacing back and forth above us."

"Jeez," Dee said.

"I was thinking maybe someone had broken in, but it seemed so impossible. The door to the attic was locked, the windows, too, and they were so scary high off the ground—this was an old Victorian house—the burglar would have had to have a crane to get in."

"So you didn't call the police?"

"We talked about it, but no, we didn't, and that's just as well. When I unlocked the attic and searched it the next morning, there was no one there. Nothing had been disturbed, the windows were still locked."

"Quite a ghost story," Dee said. "Wanna hear mine."

"Yeah," Charlie said, "but later—we're here."

CHAPTER 24

WHEN HE SAW THE SMOKE curling through the trees, Paulie quickly finished busing the last of the breakfast dishes, lugged them to the sink, tugged off his apron, and set about filling a platter with leftovers from the grill: misshapen pancakes, burnt home-fries, near-desiccated sausages, a slab of scrapple looking as gray as death, and a mound of grits, white as maggots. Monroe, who was well aware of Paulie's "friend in the forest," added three fresh-cooked eggs, over easy, to the crowded platter and topped it all off with a generous splash of syrup.

"You shouldn't be doin' this," Monroe offered. "He'll never move on, and you'll be stuck with him."

"No, he's moving on," Paulie said. "Says he's just got to finish some serious business, is all."

"Serious business?" Monroe scoffed. "Let me tell you somethin', boy. This plate of food here is the *only* serious business he'll be doin' today."

Paulie took the platter from Monroe and draped a paper napkin over it, adding a couple of dried-out, weapons-grade biscuits to hold it down. "He's just down on his luck, is all."

"Luck?" Monroe said, his eyes growing wide. "Boy, you make your own luck in this world, and don't you forget it. You sit around waitin' for somethin' good to happen, and life'll just roll over you—like him out there in the woods. You want that for yourself, huh?"

Paulie had heard this lecture before, so he responded as he usually did—"whatever"—and headed for the woods and the beckoning column of smoke, leaving Monroe standing there, shaking his head at the plum-foolishness of youth. But when he turned back to the grill and began scraping it to make way for the burgers and steaks and onions that would surely sizzle there all afternoon and well into the evening, he thought of a particularly ripe plum from his own youth, a memory that set him to giggling, then erupting into window-rattling laughter.

"Lord, lord, lord . . ."

CHAPTER 25

TO SAY THAT DEE AND CHARLIE were startled by what they saw when Grace opened the door, or that Grace was not equally startled, would have been an understatement of biblical proportions.

Charlie was startled to see Grace standing there in a blouse that almost wasn't there, her breasts near bursting out, aureoles peeking out, pinkly resplendent half-moons, nipples erect. Dee was startled by this sight as well, going from wide-eyed wonder to squint-eyed anger in an instant: *Stay away from my man, bitch!* And Grace, who was perhaps the most startled of the three, not expecting that bitch-waitress to be standing there next to Charlie, her fingers interlaced with his in the unmistakable handshake of love, quickly tugged at her blouse, trying to cover up, but the blouse just wouldn't cooperate. It had one setting: full open.

"Sorry," Grace said sheepishly. "Hadn't quite finished getting dressed."

"You think?" Dee said.

"No problem," Charlie said, staring at her breasts, which earned him a finger-breaking squeeze from Dee.

"Yeah, no problem at all," said Dee. "You look just fine, really."

Fine was not what Grace read in Dee's expression.

"Let me just get a sweater," she said, turning her back to them and darting for the bedroom. "Make yourselves comfortable, I'll only be a minute, have some coffee and croissants."

Charlie and Dee came into the apartment and walked down the short entry hall to the living room. The place looked like something out of *Architectural Digest*, everything just so, furniture, carpets, paintings, lamps, floral arrangements—everything—counterpoint to each other, color playing on color, texture on texture, a delight to the eye. And in the center of all this, two opposing loveseats, fiery red, a glass-topped coffee table between them set for two, a steaming silver teapot in the center, flanked by a silver creamer and sugar set and a stack of scones and croissants nestled in a blue-cloth napkin within a silver-latticed basket. A nearby dish brimmed with strawberry preserves, and on either end of the table rosewood-scented candles, sweet and woody, flickered in cut crystal holders. The stereo, barely audible, there but not there, filled the room with whispered jazz, soft and mellow, the base deep and thrumming, the heartbeat of the room. All the scene needed now was Grace, draped across a loveseat, sleek as a panther on the prowl in those tight-fitting slacks and that blouse, parted like The Red Sea, breasts heaving waves of alabaster, to complete the effect: *seduction*.

CHAPTER 26

GRACE'S TRANSFORMATION FROM SEXY to frumpy was highlighted by a gray sweatshirt with the message *Fear the Turtle* embossed in red across the front, along with the image of an angry, anthropomorphic terrapin poised for a fight, a fight that must have come and gone long ago judging from the lightness of the image, which had nearly flecked away from repeated washings. The slacks, tight fitting to the point of anatomical detail, had been replaced by baggy sweatpants, like the sweatshirt, old and faded.

Grace, too, seemed faded now, her makeup roughly washed away in the two minutes that she'd been gone, revealing wrinkles never suspected, like viewing the surface of the moon up close. And then there were the glasses, horn-rimmed and long out of style, poised on her nose, a librarian's chain drooping down from either side and looping around her neck, the better to prevent their disappearance through forgetfulness or the occasional gale-force winds.

Dee seemed satisfied by this transformation, giving Grace an acknowledging but icy nod as she re-entered the room, a look that seemed to say, *there, that's better now*. But the transformation, if anything, had the opposite effect on Charlie, who preferred cotton to lace, and knew that under those sweats was a braless woman in a thong, who minutes earlier had clearly expressed her intentions toward him. As much as he loved Dee—and the word *love* came easily now, no longer sounding alien—he was mesmerized by Grace, and at the same time, angered by her, an emotion that steadily overpowered him.

Grace dropped down on the couch opposite them, curled her legs up Indian style, and without preamble, launched into the subject at hand: ghosts.

"We didn't *want* to believe it at first, Bill and I. I mean, it sounds so ridiculous. *Ghosts?* And they seemed so real and sweet and vulnerable, and their pies—well, you know about the pies . . ."

"That's one of my questions," Dee said. "Those pies, there's something odd about them, you know, and—"

"But that's not the *first* question," Charlie interrupted, anger growing in him. "The first question is, Why in god's name didn't you tell me about this *before* I bought the diner?"

Grace winced, tears welling quickly in her eyes. "I . . . I thought . . . it was over," she stammered.

Her tears completely disarmed Charlie, but not so Dee.

"Oh, come *on*, Grace," she said, annoyed. "You knew—*knew*—that they'd followed that diner regardless of the owner. It's all there in those damn news clippings, right from the beginning, with what's-his-name . . ."

"Davis," Charlie offered. "The first owner."

"Exactly," Dee said. "And I think that custom wall has something to do with it, but I have no idea why."

Mention of the wall made Grace look up and give Dee a quizzical look. How could she know?

"I do," Grace said, wiping away her tears with the back of her hand. "I checked that out—afterwards."

"So . . . what's that all about?" Charlie said, calmer now, his anger abating.

Grace looked over at him and offered a brief smile of contrition. "Oh, it's about *everything*, is all. Davis got his hands on the land cheap. There was even a diner on the site then, but it was really nothing more than a burned out shell, so he bought a new one . . ."

"With that custom wall," Dee said.

"Yes, with a wall to block the view."

"Of what?" Charlie said.

Grace glanced back and forth at them. "Of a *cemetery*," she said.

Dee's jaw dropped. "Well, hello, ghosts."

"But I still don't get it," Charlie said. "Why would they haunt *my* diner?"

"Good question," Grace said. "The thing is, it's not about *your* diner, or at least I don't think so. I think it's about the other one, the one that Davis had hauled off for scrap . . ."

Charlie and Dee leaned forward, expectant, as Grace paused to gauge their reaction before continuing.

"There was a tragedy. It was a Saturday night and the diner, *The Bluebird Diner*, an old Worcester from the 1930s, was packed with locals who'd apparently come straight from the county fair to celebrate something or other. Anyway, a fight broke out. Witnesses, some late-arriving celebrants in the parking lot, said they saw two men and a woman fighting over a little girl inside the diner. A gun was drawn, shots were fired, and apparently one of the shots hit the propane tank. Everyone inside was killed—more than fifty people—near incinerated. The blast was heard three towns away."

"Wow," Charlie said. "That's terrible."

"Shit," Dee said, shaking her head.

"Yeah, and forensics being what they were back then, it was impossible to identify the remains. So . . . the town buried all of them in a mass grave just inside the cemetery wall, a stone's throw from the diner."

"So Davis put in the wall . . ." Dee said.

"To block the view," Grace said, "so town's people would not be reminded of the tragedy."

"But it seems to have pissed off the ghosts," Charlie said.

Dee near snorted. "I'll say."

Charlie threw up his hands. "But why . . . why out of all those people, are just Martha, Mindy, and Heph haunting my diner?"

"Makes sense to me," Dee said. "They were the ones fighting, right?"

Grace sighed heavily. "I don't think you guys quite understand what's going on . . ."

CHAPTER 27

JEANIE TOOK A QUICK HEADCOUNT of the customers at the counter, assessing the needs of each for coffee refills or checks, keeping a sharp eye out for tips, hoping for folding green when even coins were in short supply, as if her customers had all just completed a master's-level course in frugality.

They were a strange lot these customers, somber and quiet and given to sideways glances at their stool mates, right and left, and to straight-ahead peering into the shimmering stainless steel that lined the walls behind the counter, trying to make out the ghostly, distorted images of people moving behind them.

Jeanie had encountered many strange customers in her time, but these regulars—if she could call them that after the few days the diner had been open—took the cake, or rather the pie. Try as she might to engage them in conversation—and her gift for gab was considerable—she rarely got past the weather with them, or more likely, the arrival time for the next batch of pies, which was answerable, but not with any precision. When the last slice of pie was gone, within minutes, two figures would appear in the distance, walking along the side of the road, steaming baskets at their sides. The diner would fall quiet then, a hundred eyes watching the pair grow larger and larger, a dropped spoon as startling as an explosion.

Jeanie took their aloofness toward her as just another side effect of the rural life, where human contact was minimal and mouths were more devoted to eating than to talking. She made allowances for their clothes, too, which were anything but stylish, unless of course overalls and drab dresses were your thing. In fact, she would have almost sworn on a stack of bibles she was in another era. Chloe had clucked admonishingly at her for this, saying they were just "good, plain folks looking for a good meal without the cleanup."

Jeanie had cocked her head at this, wondering at Chloe's insouciance and worrying mightily about the fate of this child in a woman's body. Some no-account bastard would take advantage of her, leaving her knocked up in a trailer park, for sure.

Chloe was serving up the last piece of pie, the less popular sweet potato, so Jeanie reflexively glanced out the window, looking for Martha and Mindy. Instead she saw Paulie disappearing into the woods with what looked like a tray of food, heading toward a column of smoke among the trees.

"Damn," she said, "*damn!*"

"What now?" said Chloe, who was rummaging around under the counter, looking for sugar packets.

"It's that damn Paulie again, feeding that homeless guy in the woods, the one who's been pilfering food and what-not from our trash."

Chloe stood up and peered toward the woods, but Paulie was already out of sight. "Well, I think that's sweet. He's got a big heart."

"Yeah, well, sometimes I don't think he has the brains that god gave lettuce."

"You're too hard on him, Jeanie. Have you ever actually talked to him?"

"Talk to him? He turns away and makes a break for it every time I so much as look at him."

"Well, you need to corner him, like I did."

"You did not."

"Yeah, I grabbed him by the arm and forced him to help me refill the salt shakers. He's actually very sweet and—*whoa!*—praise the lord."

"Huh?"

Chloe pointed toward the road. Martha and Mindy were already crossing the parking lot with their pie-laden baskets. "Pie's a comin'," she announced loudly.

This was hardly news to the customers, who had been silently tracking the pair, their stools slowly rotating like navigational gyros to maintain a fix on them. When the pair finally entered the diner and hoisted their baskets onto the counter, all the stools squeaked in unison, spinning to face Chloe and Jeanie, who had no trouble interpreting the raised hands, some waving vigorously, or the facial expressions, a mix of desire and desperation, that all cried one unuttered but clearly heard word: *pie*.

CHAPTER 28

GRACE TOOK A SIP OF COFFEE, set down her cup, and looked from Dee to Charlie. "They're reliving that night," she said. "All of them."

The words stunned Charlie, and especially Dee, who had waited on them, served them food.

"Wait, wait . . . you're saying our customers are dead people?" she said.

"Not all, but a lot of them."

"But they eat, they drink—*shit*, they flirt with me!"

"I know," Grace said, "and I have no explanation for that—or anything, really."

Charlie didn't care whether they ate, drank, or did magic tricks, he was focused on why they were there and how to get rid of them. "So," he said, "they're reliving that night."

"Maybe *reliving* isn't the right word," Dee said.

"Yeah, right," Charlie smiled, "but they haven't really relived it, have they, at least not yet, right?" He turned to Grace. "You and Bill were in that diner for, what, two years?"

"Yeah, about that."

"Then why did they wait so long?"

"I wondered about that, too," Grace said, "and the answer is, everything has to be just right, right down to the moon."

"Huh?" Dee said. "The moon?"

"Yeah, I know it sounds weird, but the same newspaper that reported the tragedy also had a story about a Vulcan Moon that night."

"Vulcan?" Dee said. "You mean like Star Trek, Mr. Spock?"

Grace laughed despite herself. "I wish. No, it's a weather thing, named after Vulcan, the Roman god of fire and the forge. It's kind of a trick of the atmosphere that makes the moon bright red. They're completely unpredictable, and we had one the night Bill died."

"But for some reason, even with that moon, something was missing," Charlie said, "because otherwise . . ."

"We wouldn't be having this conversation," Dee said, completing his thought.

"Grace, what about Davis and the other owners, Swanson and McAllister?" Charlie said. "What happened to them?"

"All I know about McAllister is what Bill told me," Grace said, "that he'd never so much as opened the diner, kept it up on blocks for years, and looked like a man reborn when Bill took it off his hands. We thought we'd made a killing . . ."

Grace paused, reflecting on that word, and finally sighed and said, "Something happened to Becky Swanson in that diner, too. Her mother said she'd had a nervous breakdown from the pressure of operating the diner, but I think what she saw is the same thing that Davis saw. She's in a loony bin and Davis is dead, like my poor Bill."

Dee saw the tears welling in Grace's eyes again, and handed her a tissue, which she took with a grateful nod.

"So," Dee said, "the scenario repeated itself at least three times, or attempted to, and something scared McAllister so bad he never even opened the diner?"

Grace nodded. "Yes."

"Well, I don't get it," Charlie said. "You'd think killing Davis would have brought some kind of closure. Why does the scenario repeat itself?"

"I don't know," Grace said. "Maybe they *can't* come to closure, and this will just keep repeating itself with every Vulcan Moon."

"And then there's this whole issue with the neon signs," said Charlie. "Not even my sign guy can figure it out—at least he hasn't so far."

Grace looked like she'd been slapped. "The signs? Don't tell me, they're flickering and buzzing insanely—impossibly."

"Exactly," said Charlie.

"Our lights did that, too, right up until Bill died. Then they went black."

"Now *that's* creepy," said Dee.

Charlie shook his head. "Remind me to enjoy flickering lights. At least they're still doing *something*."

"Yeah," said Dee, but like you said, Charlie, maybe something's missing," Dee said. "Maybe they haven't really completed a single scenario . . . you know, because some little detail isn't right."

"Maybe," Grace said. "But what?"

Dee shrugged. "Yeah, what?"

"Well," Charlie said, "one thing missing is Martha's husband. *Two* men and a woman were fighting just before the explosion, remember? So where's he?"

"Maybe one of the customers . . ." Dee offered.

"Maybe," Grace said, "but wouldn't Martha and Mindy interact with him?"

"Yeah," Charlie said. "Those two don't really interact with the customers."

"Got it!" Dee said, clapping her hands together. "Maybe Davis and Bill were substitutes for her husband."

"Huh?" Charlie said.

"You know," Dee continued, "maybe her husband owned that diner, and for whatever reason, killing the diner's owner is part of the scenario." She reflected on that and then said, "Shit, that would mean . . ."

Grace and Dee looked at Charlie, who was already nodding his head.

"Makes sense," he said, "and it fits with what Mindy told Pearl, that they wanted to kill me."

"No, that *can't* be it," Dee said, no longer willing to accept her own theory. "I must be wrong. *No,* there's something else missing, is all. We just have to find her husband."

Charlie reached over and rubbed her shoulder. "Maybe, but better safe than sorry. Let's assume I'm the target."

They sat there silently a moment, and then Grace said, "At any rate, this whole scenario thing could go on for months, even years. It's not like we don't have time to figure it out."

"Unless we look up and see a red moon tonight," Dee said.

"Wait a minute," Charlie said. "Maybe it won't happen—*ever.*"

"What?" Grace said.

"Look, I've already chased off Heph. Why not do the same thing with Martha and Mindy?"

Dee seemed cheered by that, but Grace was shaking her head.

"Bill thought that, too," she said, "but when the moon turned red, they were all there . . ."

Dee stood up and started pacing. "Well, we have to do *something*."

"All right, then," Grace said. "Shut it down, walk away, I'll refund your money, Charlie."

Charlie considered the offer, but only briefly. Maybe it was pure stubbornness, but he couldn't walk away from his diner, his dream. And if he had to get through a nightmare to realize his dream, then so be it.

"No," he said firmly.

"But Charlie, we could—"

"*No!* I'm *not* walking away from this. There *must* be some way to end this."

"Like what," Dee snorted, "ask them for the script?"

Charlie smiled at her and shrugged. "Yeah, why not?"

"You're not *serious*," Dee said.

"Of course I am," he said. "I'll confront Martha, see what I can find out—and send the ghosts packing. Come on, Dee, let's get back to the diner."

"Is there anything I can do, Charlie?" Grace said.

"Yes, if you don't mind."

"Anything."

"Okay, could you check out who owned The Bluebird Diner?"

"Sure, I'll get right on it." She walked them to the door. "Charlie, if it doesn't work out, though, my offer stands. Please give it some serious thought. I never intended this to happen and I don't want you to get hurt." She looked over at Dee. "Either of you."

"I know that," Charlie said, "but no thanks, I can't walk away from this."

"Then be careful," she said.

After they had left, she walked over to the bookshelf and pulled out a binder long neglected, her and Bill's photo album. The tears came swiftly, uncontrollably.

CHAPTER 29

THE FIRST COUPLE OF MINUTES on the drive to the diner, Charlie and Dee didn't speak, each reflecting on the conversation with Grace.

"So, what's your ghost story?" Charlie said, breaking the silence, hoping that would provide a distraction.

"Oh, nothing," Dee said. "Anyway, not as good as yours."

"No, tell me, Dee, I really want to hear it."

"Okay." She collected her thoughts for a moment and then launched into the story.

"It's really a simple story. My father was a self-employed upholsterer who did his work in a dilapidated, leaky, and slightly tilting shed he'd built behind the house. How the thing stood up is a miracle.

"Anyway, one morning, while I was sitting in the kitchen eating my usual teenage breakfast of grape soda and donuts, I saw my father come bursting out of the shed, which was startling on two counts. First, I had never seen a look of fear on his face—I mean, *never*—and second, he was running, something he never did.

"So with my mouth open in mid-chew, jelly oozing from my lips, I watched him vault onto the back steps and burst into the kitchen, yelling my mother's pet name, *Nuisance*."

Charlie laughed. "Sorry, but *Nuisance?*"

"Yeah, I know," Dee said, giggling. "Anyway, Nuisance—aka Dorothy, Dickie, and Mom—jumped up from her sewing machine and met him in the kitchen. She did her best to calm him down, but he was like freaking."

"So what happened in the shed?"

"Well, he said he'd been working on a sofa and happened to glance over at his workbench, where a hammer was rising into the air and floating toward him."

"Whoa."

"Yeah, it freaked him out, and it gave me goose bumps. But my mom just laughed at him, which was her normal reaction to most things—emergencies, problems, finances, any conflict, she'd just try to laugh them off. Anyway, while he waited in the kitchen, peering at us through the window, Mom and I went to the shed to check it out. Of course, we found nothing. No floating hammers, much to her relief—and my disappointment. I really wanted to see that floating hammer, but everything was quiet, except for the sound of figs dropping onto the tin roof and rolling off."

She smiled at Charlie. "God, I loved those summers, the smell of those figs. Anyway, many years later, on the day he died, he claimed to see an angel with brown wings—brown, can you imagine— standing in the corner of his hospital room, smiling at him and holding that very same hammer. My mother laughed."

Her voice trailed off. They drove on silently.

CHAPTER 30

EVEN THOUGH "ONE HOUR" HAD TURNED into more than two because of traffic, Jesus's smile could not have been broader or friendlier when Charlie and Dee finally walked through the door, Dee scurrying off to talk to Chloe and Jeanie.

Charlie returned Jesus's smile and said, "why don't you head on home, Jesus, I'll take it from here."

"Gladly," Jesus sighed. He tugged off his apron, tucked it under the counter, and was gone.

Charlie turned his attention to Dee, who was at the other end of the counter talking animatedly to Chloe and Jeanie, both of whom were as wide-eyed and slack-jawed as they were silent.

But when Charlie walked up to them, their silence burst not like one bubble, but like an effervescent fountain of bubbles, their whispered comments coming quickly, overlapping.

"You're joking, right?" This from Chloe, hands on hips.

"No, I *knew* it." This from Jeanie, giving Charlie a scolding look, like all this was his fault.

"But it *can't* be." Chloe again, determined not to believe, even though deep down, she really did.

"From the very first day." Omniscient Jeanie.

"Wait, wait." Charlie, holding up his hands as if bracing for the charge of wild animals.

"Didn't I *tell* you, Chloe?" Jeanie, ignoring Charlie, presenting her evidence to the jury.

"What?" Chloe, Jeanie's straight-man.

"Remember, that batch of pies they made in less than an hour—*impossible!*" Jeanie rests her culinary case.

"Yeah, I guess." Chloe, coming around.

"Guess nothin', they're *ghosts* for sure." Jeanie, too loudly, customers' heads turning.

"*Shh!*" Charlie, Dee, and Chloe ganging up on Jeanie, returning their customers' gazes with forced smiles. *Nothin' goin' on here, folks, move along.*

Finally, Charlie regained some semblance of control, issuing orders to each to, *one*, spread the word—quietly—to the rest of the staff, and *two*, keep their eyes pealed for the arrival of Martha and Mindy. And a late added *three*, be cool and let him handle them.

And so they scattered, three waitresses in the know, carrying their message to the others and setting down the rules of engagement. Deuce, interrupted as he bused a table, struck a pose he knew would highlight his biceps, paying more attention to the intended effect it was having on a pretty girl in a corner booth than on the message whispered in his ear, winking at the girl while shrugging at the message.

"That's bullshit," he said, moving away, much to the chagrin of Chloe, who pursued him to the kitchen.

Paulie, on the other hand, greeted the news with proper alarm, nodding vigorously to the rules, giving Jeanie a thumbs up and moving away to bus a table, leaving her shaking her head, bemused. She'd expected her ghost feeder to balk at the news, even be upset or defiant, but he greeted the news as if his care and feeding of a ghost had never happened. *That boy is just plain weird,* Jeanie thought.

Monroe laughed more heartily than usual when Dee whispered in his ear, customers turning their heads, wondering what joke she had told him. Then he was silent, seeing the seriousness and resolve in her eyes and feeling her grip on his arm tightening. He nodded slowly to everything she said, then went back to work, flipping burgers and frying onions, occasionally looking back over his shoulder at the doorway, his laugh replaced by a nervous vigilance that seemed to deflate the mood of everyone, the entire diner growing quiet.

And then they came, their baskets smoking in the afternoon chill, brightening the mood of the customers as they entered, the unmistakable smell of pies filling the diner, prompting more than a few customers to tap a spoon on their mug to get the attention of Chloe or Jeanie or Dee, who ignored the growing clamor and entreaties for pie to watch Martha and Mindy's progress to the counter, where they unveiled each pie, lifting them out of the baskets with a reverence only churchgoers could quite understand. And when they were done, Martha looked around for Charlie, who was sitting in the back booth, pretending *not* to notice her. Spotting him, she grabbed Mindy's hand, tugged her to the booth, and gave her a gentle nudge into the seat opposite Charlie before sitting down herself. Behind her, the diner erupted with requests for *pie, pie, pie,* Jeanie and Chloe and Dee serving it up as quickly as they could while keeping curious eyes on Charlie's booth.

"Afternoon, Charlie," Martha said, her look bright, expectant, though Charlie couldn't think why.

"Hi," he said to her, and then turned to Mindy. "And how are *you* today, Mindy?"

Mindy frowned, eyes narrowing. "Fine." Her voice was flat, unenthusiastic.

"So," Martha said, "did you talk to him?"

Him? And then it hit Charlie. "Oh, oh, you mean Heph? Yes, I talked to him, sent him away."

Martha beamed at him and reached over and gave Mindy a little hug, which Mindy shrugged off. "I don't believe you. If he's gone, why's there smoke in the woods?"

Charlie glanced out the window and saw the telltale smoke. "*Damn,* I guess I'll have to have another talk with him."

"Won't do no good because—"

"Mindy!" Martha scolded, but Mindy would not be hushed.

"It's true, you know it's—"

"Shush, now," Martha said, slamming a fist down so hard the salt and pepper shakers launched themselves into the air and clattered off the table, attracting the attention of everyone, particularly Dee and Chloe and Jeanie, who had been watching the goings on in the booth intently.

Mindy, silenced but seething, pantomimed the zipping and locking of her lips, the invisible key tossed over her shoulder, and went into a steely, cross-armed pout.

Martha, satisfied, unballed her fists and turned back to Charlie, who had been studying both of them. They seemed so real, and try as he might, he could not see through them. How did Pearl manage that?

"So, you'll talk to him, *again?*" she said, her voice quavering.

Charlie nodded. "And if that doesn't work, I'll get the police to roust him out."

"Good," she said absently, her eyes drifting, taking in the diner and its customers, some of whom gave her acknowledging nods. *Shit*, Charlie thought, *I hadn't noticed that before*.

"Looks like you're doing good business. I best be heading home, make some pies."

She started to get up, but Charlie stopped her.

"Wait a second, I need to talk to you."

She sat back in the seat. "About the pies? Don't worry about that, we'll—"

"No, about you and Mindy!" He had raised his voice. A few customers—ghosts?—already alarmed by the fist-slamming, spun on their stools once again to see what was going on, then just as quickly spun back to sip their coffee and finish their pie.

Martha looked taken aback, yet retained a look of pure innocence. "Why, whatever about?"

"About that night at The Bluebird Diner."

Martha gasped and Mindy broke her silence. "You leave my momma alone," she said forcefully, poking a finger at Charlie.

Martha reached out and pulled Mindy's arm down. "Charlie, what in the world are you talking about?"

"About you, about Mindy, and the others," he said. "You all died that night in The Bluebird."

If ghosts can be said to blanch, Martha and Mindy did just that, but just as quickly recovered, Mindy giving Charlie a steely, withering look, Martha solemn, nodding her head and saying, "Yes, I guess you could say that. Losing a husband, a father, *is* like dying."

"No," Charlie said, "I mean you *are* dead, *literally*—you're ghosts!" He whispered the word again. "Ghosts."

Martha began laughing nervously. "Oh, Charlie, you are too funny. I'm as alive as anyone here."

Charlie shook his head. "Some maybe, but no, no you're not, and I want *both* of you, *all* of you, *out* of my diner—*now!*—and never come back."

"Can't stop us," Mindy blurted out, eyes narrowed, leveled on Charlie.

This time Martha didn't shush her, but turned on Charlie. "You *can't* be serious. That's crazy talk. *Me* dead? *Mindy* dead? Absurd. Here, take my hand, does *that* feel dead to you?"

Charlie refused to take it. "And where's that husband of yours? Is he here? Which one is he?"

"My husband? What's wrong with you?"

"There's nothing wrong with—"

"It's that damn man in the woods, isn't it. Fillin' your head with lies, nonsense, pure foolishness."

"No, it's—"

"Well, you have a good talk with that Heph person," she said. "Maybe *he's* the one's dead. I sure would like that."

"Me, too!" Mindy snapped.

Martha grabbed Mindy's arm and pulled her out of the booth. "Come along, child, we *ghosts* have to make some pies for these hungry folks."

"No more pies!" Charlie yelled out after them as they near ran for the door, his words startling the customers, who gaped at him like he was deranged.

Charlie slumped back into the booth. "Well, *that* went well," he mumbled to himself.

CHAPTER 31

"IT DOESN'T SEEM TO BE GOING ALL THAT WELL," Jeanie said to Chloe. They were watching Charlie talk to Martha and Mindy and could tell just from their expressions that the conversation was going anything *but* well.

"You think?" Chloe said. "Man, those girls are madder than wet hens."

Jeanie laughed. "Sounds like something I'd say, Chloe dear. So, what do you think of all this ghost stuff?"

Chloe shrugged. "Oh, I don't know. I guess I'm not all that frightened. I mean, I've seen a ghost before."

"Really?"

"Yeah, when I was just a little girl. First time I saw him, it scared me big time, but then I kind of looked forward to his visits."

"Visits?"

"Well, I guess they weren't visits, because I think he was there all the time, but I only saw him in one place at one time. I'd keep the door to my bedroom open just to see him. He'd walk by every night, carrying a bucket. He looked like a farmer, so maybe he was getting water or about to milk a cow. Whatever he was up to, he carried that bucket past my door every night for as long as I lived there. My parents never saw a thing, though. It was all very weird and yet, I don't know, comforting in a way, like it was right and proper that he be there every night. When I moved away and got my apartment last year, I really missed him."

"Well, if that don't beat all," Jeanie said.

"So, how about you, Jeanie. Seen any ghosts?"

Jeanie shook her head. "No, never have, but my sister claims to see them every day, especially our grandmother, who's been dead going on ten years." Jeanie began chuckling.

"What?" Chloe said, giggling too.

"She claims that every day when she gets home from work, grandma is there to nag her about a window she broke in grandma's house fifty years ago. Says grandma is a regular pain in the ass, pardon my French."

"Speaking of pains in the-you-know-what," Chloe said, "there they go."

Jeanie and Chloe watched as Martha near dragged Mindy out of the diner.

CHAPTER 32

THINGS HAD BEEN GOING WELL FOR GRACE. She had only to call her lawyer, Johnny Shark, to set things in motion. Shark responded to her request with a blasé, "no problemo, gimme a few hours."

For Grace, that meant a few hours spent pampering herself, bathing, painting her nails, fussing with her hair and makeup, choosing just the right clothes to wear for her next meeting with Charlie, something alluring but more subtle and sedate, a look that even Dee would find non-threatening. *She may have her hooks in him*, Grace thought, *but she hasn't reeled him in, at least not yet, judging from the look he gave me when I opened the door.*

When Shark called, she was sitting on the couch, her feet on the coffee table, cotton balls between her toes.

"Sorry it took so long," he said, "but getting *anything* out of those bureaucrats down at city hall, well, it's like pulling—"

"What did you find out?" she said, holding the phone with one hand, leaning forward and removing the cotton balls with the other.

"Okay, okay, here's the deal. The last owner of The Bluebird Diner was a Chester McAllister . . . ."

"*What?*" she said, almost dropping the phone. "That's *impossible*. McAllister is the guy we bought *our* diner from. The owner of The Bluebird was killed when the diner exploded."

"Exploded? Dead? What are you talking about? All I know is what's written in black and white down at city hall, plus . . ."

"Plus? Plus what?"

"Plus, I did a little follow-up, so I can tell you where to find him, if need be."

"Oh, there's a need, all right."

Grace scribbled the information on a slip of paper and ended the call with a quick, "Thanks, bye."

Fifteen minutes later, she was on the phone with Charlie, who was as dumbstruck as Grace to learn that the man who had sold the diner to Grace's husband was the same man who had owned The Bluebird.

"We've got to talk with him," Charlie said.

"Way ahead of you, Charlie. I just got off the phone with him. He's in a nursing home about thirty minutes from here, and he's agreed to see us. Can I swing by and pick you up?"

Charlie didn't hesitate. "Oh, absolutely."

The nursing home, a two-story brick building as uninspired in design as a shoebox, reeked of antiseptic, dead flowers, and urine. Its hallways, freshly waxed bowling alleys of speckled gray linoleum, were filled with wheelchairs, gurneys, and the nursing home's staff, mostly scurrying nurses in scrubs of disconcertingly bright colors—greens and purples and blues—making them look more like moving popsicles than people. McAllister's room, a white box with two hospital beds separated by a pale green privacy curtain, especially reeked of urine, no doubt the uncontrollable output of McAllister and his roommate, an unseen man snoring loudly on the other side of the curtain. Charlie and Grace stepped back into the hallway at the first whiff of it, then steeled themselves, and entered.

McAllister, propped up in bed, sheets neatly tucked at his waist, looked like a man long dead, his body skeletal and shrunken, his skull clearly evident, skin near transparent, sagging in waves from his eyes, which were hollow and red-rimmed and dead-blue, as if they had seen enough of life and had passed on to another plane where curiosity and emotion held no purchase.

"You them?" he said, voice rasping.

They nodded.

"Can't offer you a seat. This damn place's got nothin'. Penny-pinchin' bastards . . . ."

"That's okay," Charlie said.

"Yeah, standing's fine," Grace said, thinking *all the better to get the hell out of here fast.* She knew she'd have to change her clothes immediately, that wretched smell insinuating itself into the fabric as quickly and as surely as cigarette smoke.

McAllister looked Grace up and down. "What's a looker like you want from an old geezer like me," he clucked, then coughed, depositing something best left unseen into a tissue, examining it briefly, as if there were something to be divined from its color or viscosity, and then tightly balling up the tissue in his hand.

Grace took one step closer to the bed. "You sold my husband a diner once, a long while back."

McAllister squinted at her, then rolled his eyes to the ceiling, searching for the handle of a memory. "So I did. A Mr. Sparks, kind of on the short side, a stump of a man, but with biceps like softballs . . . ."

"Not Sparks, *Sharp*, Bill Sharp."

McAllister frowned. "You sure about that?"

"Yes, I'm his widow, Grace Sharp."

The word *widow* alarmed him, his eyes going wide, jaw dropping, revealing a dentist's nightmare of yellowed teeth. "He's *dead?*"

"Yes, a heart attack, in the diner, but—"

"But what we really want to talk to you about," Charlie said, "is The Bluebird."

McAllister froze for a moment, then slumped back in bed as if a great burden had once again landed on him, pressing him down. "Don't tell me . . . *damn it all* . . . they're back, aren't they, them ghosts?"

"Yes," Charlie said. "Big time."

"Can you tell us about that last night at The Bluebird?" Grace said. "We're looking for a clue—anything—that might help us put a stop to this once and for all."

McAllister lay there, shaking his head. "I wish I could," he said, "but I wasn't there. Went home sick that afternoon, a bad case of the trots—not the kind of thing you want your customers to see, or smell, if you get my drift."

Charlie and Grace did, and nodded.

"So, I was home, sittin' on the you-know-what," he continued, "when the explosion near knocked me off the pot . . . and I was a mile away at that. Time I got there, it was an inferno. Town's only fire truck spraying it down with water . . . totally useless, like pissin' on a bonfire. People standin' around in shock, helpless, crying, all lookin' at me like it was my fault . . . ."

His voice trailed off and he grew silent, eyes closed, his thoughts clearly turned inward, reliving the moment. Then he looked up at them, his jaw set, firm.

"But what I *can* tell you is what happened next . . . and then maybe you can tell me what in hell's been goin' on . . . ."

CHAPTER 33

THE DAY WORE ON TO LATE AFTERNOON, the staff vigilant, nervous, but if anything, the diner was as calm as it had ever been—no disputes over correct change, no coffee spills, no dropped trays of dishes, no wrongly filled orders, no trash talking from Jesus or Monroe, the customers and staff filling their appointed roles without complaint or incident. Even the pie was plentiful enough to keep everyone happy.

Pearl arrived just before the evening rush, carrying her backpack of school work to Charlie's booth and starting on her homework assignments under the watchful eye of Dee, who took time between customers to check her progress and whisper encouragement.

"Momma," Pearl said, looking up from a sheet of math problems, "did Charlie chase them away?"

Dee sighed. "No child, but he tried."

Pearl quickly looked around to see if Martha and Mindy were anywhere to be seen. "You don't think they'll come *tonight*, do you?"

Dee glanced over at the pie cases, where three whole pies and two partials sat. "No, I expect not. We have plenty of pie. Besides, if they do show up, ain't no way I'll let you come to harm."

"Thanks, momma," she said, smiling briefly, then growing somber. "Momma?"

"What is it, honey?"

"Lucinda said a ghost near killed her."

Oh, god, Dee thought. *Not Lucinda again.* Lucinda of the gross exaggeration. Lucinda of the sky is falling. She could picture Lucinda pulling Pearl aside, eyes growing wider and wider as she piled lie upon lie to scare her little girl. "Honey, I bet Lucinda's never even seen a ghost, let alone—"

"But she has, momma, she has. I didn't tell her about the flicker, but she described it to me."

"Really?" Maybe this time, this one time, Lucinda was telling the truth. Pearl was nodding vigorously. "Okay, then, tell me about it."

Lucinda had told Pearl she'd been at a sleepover at her friend Marie's a year ago, a month before she met Pearl. After the usual pizza and pillow fights, the girls had finally settled down, each staking out her territory for sleep. Lucinda, who not unsurprisingly to Dee, had been one of the last to settle down, was relegated to the floor, along with several other girls. About an hour later, as Lucinda dreamed of riding a sleek silver fish in an emerald green sea—*god, how she could embellish things!*—she was awakened by a young boy who had grabbed her by both ankles and was pulling her across the floor toward the fireplace, which was still roaring. Her first thought was to laugh, thinking the boy must be one of Marie's brothers. But then she saw the look in his eyes, an evil look she had never seen before, and she just started screaming.

"And that's when she saw him flicker, momma," Pearl said.

Dee nodded. "I believe you, honey. Then what?"

"He kept pulling her toward the fire, saying, 'You're mine now, you're mine.' But her screams saved her. The other girls woke up. Now, they couldn't see the boy at all, but what they did see was Lucinda sliding across the floor on her back, screaming, both legs impossibly in the air.

"So they began screaming, too, and grabbing at Lucinda's arms, stopping her just before her legs went into the fire."

Pearl paused, tears filling her eyes. "Something like that's not going to happen to me, is it?"

Dee pulled her close and gave her a hug. "Of course not, child. Charlie and I will protect you."

Pearl nodded and wiped away her tears. "Okay . . . okay."

Dee smiled down at her and gave her another squeeze. "Okay, then, back to that math homework. Need any help?"

Pearl smiled weakly, then nodded. "Yeah, this advanced math is *hard*."

"Don't think of it as hard," Dee said. "Think of it as *challenging*."

"You mean like getting rid of ghosts?"

Dee chuckled. "Yeah, just like that, but we'll overcome, don't you doubt that. Meanwhile, let's tackle that math problem."

"Okay."

Pearl looked down at her paper and read aloud: "If a train leaves Baltimore traveling south at 50 mph at the same time another train leaves Washington traveling north at 75 mph, how many miles from Washington will the two trains meet, considering that the distance between Washington and Baltimore is 37 miles?"

Dee groaned. "Maybe you had it right the first time, Pearl. That's *hard*."

Pearl giggled. "Yeah, and why would anyone need to know that?"

"I don't know. I guess it's important to somebody, though."

Pearl grew serious. "Momma?"

Oh, no, Dee thought. *Not another ghost story.* "Yeah, Pearly? What's wrong?"

"Do you mind if I never take a train ride between Baltimore and Washington?"

Dee laughed out loud and wagged a finger at a giggling Pearl. "You *got* me with that one, for sure."

Pearl tossed her pencil down on the paper and rested her head in her hands. "Whew, this stuff makes my head hurt."

"That's homework for you," Dee said.

"Ought a be a law . . ."

"Oh, come on, it's not *that* bad."

Pearl looked up at Dee and shoved the paper across the booth toward her. "Oh, yeah? Then *you* do it."

"Ha! Nice try, but it's *your* homework."

Pearl grudgingly pulled the paper back and picked up the pencil. "That Mindy is lucky."

"What?"

"I mean, she doesn't have to do any homework. All she has to do is make magic pies and go all transparent and flickery and stuff."

Dee suppressed a laugh but couldn't help grinning. "There is that *downside*, though."

"Huh?"

"Being dead and all."

"Oh, that. Yeah, I guess, but wouldn't it be cool to go near invisible like that?"

Dee had to admit it would be cool. "Like to avoid some of my customers? Oh, yeah."

"You know what, though?" Pearl said, serious now. "I don't think she can control it."

"What do you mean?"

"When I saw through her, it was just for a second, like Lucinda saw, a flicker, and it was because I snuck up behind her and scared her. She like lost control."

"Humph," Dee said, looking around at the customers, trying to sort out which would flicker if she walked up behind them and shouted *boo!*

"Now *that's* gotta be cool, a person scaring a ghost."

Pearl beamed. "You know what, maybe if they come back, we should just walk up to them and go *boo!*"

Dee reached across the table and rubbed Pearl's head. "You *are* a ghostbuster!"

Pearl, giggling, returned to her homework, Dee watching in wonder as her little girl started filling the paper with equations. *What we need now*, Dee thought, *is a ghost equation.*

CHAPTER 34

"I WAS DESTITUTE," MCALLISTER BEGAN, "inconsolable." He reached for a tissue and dabbed it delicately at each eye, like an actor putting the finishing touches on his makeup.

"Well, of course," Grace said. "Your diner, all those people . . . gone."

"I became a ghost to everyone in that town after that; couldn't show my face during the day—despite my loss—so I'd only venture out at night, and always to the diner. Sometimes, I thought if I just blinked my eyes, hard, the diner would reappear, whole, and life would go on . . ."

He paused and looked back and forth at Charlie and Grace, chewing on his next words before speaking. "But it didn't."

"What *did* happen?" Charlie asked.

"They came . . ." McAllister said, his voice almost a whisper.

"The ghosts?" Grace said.

"Yes, the ghosts. I was standing there in the dark like always, nothin' but the moon for light, staring at my burned out diner . . . and they came, looking whole as you and me, from that damned graveyard. I near keeled over right then and there, I was tremblin' so. To see those people I *knew* and *loved* . . ."

"What did they do when they saw you?" Charlie asked.

"They didn't see me at first. They were focused on the diner, walking around in what was left of her anyway, some of them wailing, some drop-jawed speechless. And then . . ."

McAllister closed his eyes, squeezing out tears that ran down his cheeks and dropped to his shirt. "And then they saw me. And they were mad, the lot of them, shaking their fists and screaming at me, all but Martha and Mindy, of course."

"*Of course?*" Grace said. "Why weren't they angry, too?"

McAllister looked at her like she was crazy. "Well, why *would* they be?" he said. "They loved me . . ."

"Loved you?" Charlie said, confused.

"My *wife*, my *child*," McAllister said. "Of course they loved me."

CHAPTER 35

THEY WERE IN DEEP THOUGHT and almost halfway back to the diner before Grace broke the silence.

"Whew, I didn't see that coming."

"Yeah," Charlie said, "but now we know."

"Do we? Just because Martha and Mindy beckoned him to come into the diner night after night doesn't necessarily mean . . ."

"That it's always the owner they're after?"

"Yeah, I think it's more complicated than that, somehow, despite what he said."

Charlie reflected on McAllister's story. He'd sold the lot The Bluebird had sat on, knowing the new owner, Davis, would cart the old diner away and with it any reason for the ghosts to reappear night after night.

But it hadn't worked, and Davis had died. Then McAllister had been sure it would all end when Becky Swanson bought the new diner and moved it to Flemington, New Jersey. But he'd been wrong, the ghosts followed. When Becky tracked him down, months later, he'd bought the diner straight out from her and put it in a darkened warehouse, where he and security cameras could keep a watchful eye on it. The ghosts had returned the first few nights, though the cameras never recorded it, but then the ghostly visits had stopped abruptly. With the passing years, McAllister had become more confident that the ghosts were permanently at rest, and needing money for his declining health, he'd sold it, finally, to Bill Sharp.

"No," Charlie said. "They're following a different diner, not the one they died in. What else could it be but the owner they're after?"

Grace shook her head. "But why wouldn't that be McAllister himself? Why aren't they just haunting him?"

"I think it might have been him at first, but Martha and Mindy have not so much as uttered his name, and . . ."

"And what?"

"I don't know. The way she looks at me, like a teenager with a crush . . ."

Grace clucked. "Charlie, in case you haven't noticed, *most* women look at you that way . . . me included."

Charlie glanced over at her, then quickly looked away, not wanting to meet the look she was giving him. "So . . ." he said, trying to quickly change the subject, "your husband had biceps big as softballs."

The laugh that escaped Grace was explosive. "Ha! That McAllister had a gift for description, huh? Yeah, well, Bill *was* in good shape."

She paused and laughed, giving her head a little shake.

"What?" Charlie said.

"Oh, nothing . . ."

"No, what's that little laugh about?"

"Okay . . . We hired this busboy, Bill and I, some kid just out of high school, with like these huge biceps. The kid goaded Bill into a weight-lifting program. And it sure worked . . ."

She paused briefly as they pulled into the parking lot. "That kid was so *full* of himself," she said, shaking her head and chuckling again. "A real lady's man—even tried to hit on *me*. Boy, that Deuce was something else."

CHAPTER 36

WHEN CHARLIE TOLD GRACE ABOUT DEUCE, she shuddered, visibly shaken.

"Come on," Charlie said, "let's go in and I'll get you some coffee."

Grace quickly shook her head. "No way I'm going in there now." She restarted the engine and put the car in reverse.

"Wait," Charlie said, "let's talk then."

"No, I need to get out of here." She was trembling. "Really, I do."

"You're safe here in the car. Please, just talk to me a minute, and then you can go."

She slipped the car back into park and slumped back in her seat, dropping her hands from the wheel and letting them fall to her lap. "Okay . . . I'm sorry I'm such a mess, but—"

"I know, I know. Look, if Deuce is a ghost, maybe Chloe or Jeanie or the others are ghosts, too."

"Not Dee, though. I'd never seen her before."

"No, not Dee." *Not the way she makes love*, Charlie thought. *Unless she's a succubus.* He shook that thought off. "But what about the others?"

"Maybe. Describe them to me."

Charlie worked his way methodically through a mental list of his staff.

Lenny? No.
The other Lenny. No.
Monroe? No.

Jeanie? No.
Pualie? No.
Chloe? No.

Charlie then described the other busboys and short-order cooks, but none rang a bell with Grace.

And then he came to Jesus.

"Yes, him, the angel, the genius with the knife. Bill and I loved him . . ."

"Oh, terrific, a ghost with a knife."

"Strange, though, why just the two of them? Why isn't the whole staff here?"

Charlie shrugged. He had no idea. "Dunno, maybe they're pieces to the puzzle in some way, and the others weren't."

"I guess."

They grew silent. Finally, Grace said, "Look, I'm really tired. I'd better be heading home. If I think of anything, I'll give you a call, okay?"

"Sure," Charlie said.

He got out of the car and watched as Grace threw the car into reverse, pulled out of the parking space, and sped away up the long hill toward the college and home, the Cadillac's distinctive taillights disappearing in the growing darkness as she crested the hill.

He turned back toward the diner and looked up at the sky. A powder puff of a moon was rising over the diner, the last traces of orange disappearing from the clouds as the Earth spun away from the sun. He glanced behind him. A knee-deep fog had already formed where the parking lot met the woods and was beginning a steady march toward the diner. Charlie half expected to see Heph and a B-movie army of the living dead emerging from the fog, but let that image go. He turned back to the diner again and looked inside.

The place looked to be about half full. Dee was walking toward his corner booth, where Pearl sat beaming at her. Chloe, behind the counter, was pouring coffee for a man in a green jacket, the words *Ajax Trucking*, emblazoned in red across the back. Jeanie, lips moving silently, was saying something to a customer as she sliced into a pie. Deuce—*Deuce!*—was clearing a table, his eyes focused on a pretty girl in the next booth. And then Charlie saw Jesus standing at his station, twirling a knife, intent on his craft, not caring about the swirl around him. *What the—* Charlie thought. *Why's he back so soon?*

He glanced up at the moon again—white—and heaved a sigh of relief. Nothing would happen tonight at least.

He walked into the diner and headed for his booth. He had a lot to tell Dee.

CHAPTER 37

GRACE POURED HERSELF A GLASS of sauvignon blanc, kicked off her shoes, and slumped down on the couch opposite the television, clicking it on and punching in Channel 15 to watch the programming schedule scroll down from sitcom to infomercial to talking heads to police drama to early evening movies already in progress.

She rested the controller on her thigh and took a sip of wine, reflecting on the meeting with McAllister. It had to be him the ghosts wanted, not Charlie. They had beckoned him time and again, hadn't they? At least until he had moved the diner into that warehouse.

She looked back at the scroll—nothing on worth watching—and punched in the Weather Channel, a blond forecaster in a bright red dress too tight for her ample derriere, describing the march of a thunderstorm across Texas.

What about putting the diner in that warehouse? Had McAllister known about the Vulcan Moon? And then she thought about Deuce and Jesus. It all seemed so odd. Deuce had tried to hit on her repeatedly, but otherwise seemed harmless. Maybe he was hitting on Martha and Jesus intervened. That would be so like Jesus. He seemed to want to protect everyone from harm. She reflected on all this, but couldn't come up with a reasonable theory. Maybe

McAllister knew how they fit the puzzle. He must have known them.

She set her wine glass down, put the television on mute, and called the nursing home. It was getting late, but maybe not too late to ask him a question or two before the nurses forced darkness on him.

The phone rang four times, then a recorded voice came on announcing that the call was being transferred. The phone rang three more times, then a woman's voice came on the line. "Nursing station. How may I help you?" There was impatience in her voice.

"Look, I know it's late," Grace said, "but I'd like to talk to Chester McAllister if I could."

"I'm sorry, but that won't be possible."

"But it's important that I talk with him tonight, and I know he'd want to take the call."

There was a pause, and then the nurse said, "I'm sorry—*really*—but that won't be possible..."

"But it will only take a minute or two," Grace said, trying to be polite but insistent.

Another pause. "Are you family?"

"No, not really..."

"I probably shouldn't be telling you this, ma'am, there are rules about this."

"Rules? What do you mean?"

Yet another pause. "I'm sorry, ma'am. Mr. McAllister passed a few minutes ago..."

Grace conveyed her sorrow, then clicked off the cell phone, tossed it on the couch next to her, and glanced at the television. The woman in the Red dress—*she really needs to do something about that hair!*—said something silently, then the screen was filled with a telescopic view of the night sky, a bright red moon centermost. Grace quickly grabbed the controller and took the television off mute.

". . . as red as my dress. It's called a Vulcan Moon, a rare event, so get yourself outside and enjoy this trick of the atmosphere."

Grace leaped up and ran to the window: a red moon hovered low in the sky, a thin bank of dark clouds streaming by it on the wind.

"Shit!"

She raced back to the couch, grabbed her cell phone, and punched in Charlie's number. The phone rang and rang and then switched over to voicemail.

"Shit, Charlie!" she screamed into the phone. "There's a Vulcan Moon! Get everyone out of that diner!"

She clicked off, slipped back into her shoes, and raced for the door.

CHAPTER 38

DEE WAS SPEECHLESS. *DEUCE? JESUS? HOW COULD THAT BE?* She glanced over at Deuce, who was clearing a table nearby. He caught her looking at him, misinterpreted her interest, and winked at her. Jesus Christ, she thought, *a ghost is trying to hit on me!*

She turned away and focused her attention on Jesus, who was handing Jeanie a turkey club assembled and sliced to perfection.

"Why just them?" she whispered to Charlie.

Before he could answer, not that he *had* an answer, Pearl interrupted. "It's like on TV, right? A ghost sticks around 'cause it has unfinished business or, you know, can't accept that she's dead."

Dee smiled at her. "So we just have to point them to the light, huh?"

Pearl shrugged. "Dunno, I'm just a kid."

"Well," Charlie said, "your theory is as good as any."

"Well in that case," Pearl said, "I'd say momma and me and Monroe are in trouble."

"Why?" Dee said.

"Like on TV and in the movies, momma. Black people are always the first to die. Then I think Chloe would be next 'cause she's real pretty and has big tits."

"Pearl!" Dee said. "That's no way to talk."

"I'm just sayin'," Pearl said.

"Well that's fine, but it doesn't bring us any closer to getting rid of the ghosts," Dee said.

"Why don't you just ask them to go?" Pearl offered matter-of-factly.

Charlie tried to imagine how that might go, and shook his head. "No, I think we should watch them a bit, see how they interact with Martha and Mindy . . . and speaking of them, have they been around?"

"No," Dee said, glancing over at the pie cases, "but judging by the supply of pie, they should be here soon enough."

"Maybe you should take Pearl home," Charlie said, offering Dee his car keys.

"No way," Pearl said. "I've got these train problems to solve."

"What?"

"Her homework," Dee said, then turned to Pearl. "You can do those at home just as well, baby."

"But I don't *like* being alone," Pearl said. "Will you stay with me, momma?"

"That'd be fine," Charlie said. "The crowd's thinning out and last time I looked the moon was pure white, so nothing's going to happen tonight."

"Well, then, maybe we should just stay," Dee said.

Pearl tugged on Charlie's shirt and pointed out the window. "Look!"

Charlie and Dee looked out the window. Paulie was moving into the woods, a flashlight in one hand, a tray of food in the other. Even in the growing darkness, a pale column of smoke could be seen rising among the trees.

"What the—" Charlie said.

"Meant to tell you. Monroe says Paulie's been feedin' someone in the woods."

Heph, Charlie thought. *Damn!* "Well, we'll just *see* about that," he said, slipping out of the booth and heading for the door.

CHAPTER 39

GRACE HAD NEVER DRIVEN THE CADDY FLAT OUT, let alone flat out with a cell phone at her ear, so the one-handed, distracted ride to the diner was as harrowing for her as it was for the pedestrians, mostly college students, she'd nearly run over as she'd rocketed through the campus on her way to the long hill that led down to the diner.

She had breathed a sigh of relief when her 411 call had produced the number of the diner—she was worried the number might be too new—and a groan of frustration and anguish when the diner's phone kept ringing and ringing.

"Come on, pick up!" she screamed into the phone. And as if on cue, someone picked up.

"Red Oak Diner, Chloe speaking, how may I—"

"I need to talk to Charlie, fast!"

"What?"

"Charlie, get Charlie! *Was she dense?*

There was a pause. Chloe had apparently put the phone down. Grace could hear her asking where Charlie was, and then she was back on the line.

"He's outside somewhere. If you give me your number, I'll—"

"No time for that. How about Dee, is she there?"

"Yeah, but she's—"

"Get her on the phone!"

"Okay, okay," Chloe said, thinking *sheesh, what a bitch!*

Grace waited and waited. Each second seemed an hour. In the time it took to get Dee on the line, Grace and the Caddy had hurtled through two red lights, barely missing the honking cars that had the right-of-way. Finally, Dee came on the line.

"Hello?" Dee said, not sure who "some bitch" might be.

"Dee, thank god! It's me, Grace."

Dee could hear the urgency in her voice. "What . . . What's wrong?"

"There's a Vulcan Moon, get everyone out!"

Dee, stunned, said nothing, just stood there, frozen to the phone.

CHAPTER 40

CHARLIE STUMBLED THROUGH THE UNDERBRUSH, nearly tripping with every step as unseen vines and fallen limbs tried to bring him down, his eyes firmly fixed on Paulie's flashlight, which glowed faintly in the trees far ahead. Then he saw the fire and the silhouettes of Paulie and Heph, who was sitting by the fire, his checkered tablecloth-shawl over his shoulders to brace against the chill October evening.

As Paulie bent down to hand Heph the tray of food, Charlie burst into the little clearing.

"Son of a *bitch!*" he screamed. "I thought I told you to clear out!"

Paulie was so startled he nearly dropped the tray. Heph was equally stunned, spinning around and rising to look at Charlie, wide-eyed, scared, arms raised to defend himself.

Charlie stopped dead in his tracks. *It wasn't Heph!*

The man relaxed a bit, seeing the confusion on Charlie's face. "Name's Parsons, Bill Parsons, most people just call me Billy." He offered his hand, then let it drop to his side when Charlie ignored him.

"Billy's harmless, down on his luck. I was just trying to help, is all," Paulie said, looking down at the ground. "I'll pay for the food if that's what—"

"Where did you get that tablecloth?" Charlie said, ignoring Paulie. "And that hat."

Parsons pulled the cloth from his shoulders and the red skullcap from his head and offered them to

Charlie, being careful not to get too close to him. He didn't like the look in Charlie's eyes. There was anger there, and fear. "I didn't know these was yours. Man said for me to take 'em, and as cold as it is, I sure as hell wasn't about to turn him down, I can tell you that."

"Man? You mean Heph?"

Parsons shrugged and put the tablecloth and cap back on when Charlie made no move to take them. "Never said his name. Just said he wouldn't be needin' 'em anymore now that his luck had changed and the moon was red."

Parsons looked up at the moon. "It's red, all right, but an odd thing to say, don't you think? No matter to me, though. Hell, I was colder than a witch's tit and glad to have 'em."

Charlie had not heard a word after Parsons mentioned the red moon. He'd just looked up at the moon, gasped, and turned on his heels, running back into the trees and the darkness, racing toward the diner.

"A lot of strange folks out tonight, don't you think?" Parsons said, taking the tray away from a drop-jawed Paulie.

"I guess," said Paulie.

Parsons surveyed the tray of food. "What do we have here? Ah, meatloaf! You've done well, my boy, you've done well."

CHAPTER 41

EVERYTHING WAS HAPPENING TOO FAST for Dee. If news of the ascendant Vulcan Moon wasn't enough to send chills up and down her spine, then the sight of Martha and Mindy racing into the diner, laden with pies, being pursued by a bearded old man with a look of pure hatred on his face certainly was.

"Grace," she whispered into the phone, "they're . . . they're here. Martha. Mindy. Hephaestus."

"*Shit!*" Grace said as the Caddy went airborne at the top of the hill, the diner's neon signs coming into view, all of them flickering and flashing crazily, the Vulcan Moon, red as a weather woman's dress, hovering above, preternaturally large from a meteorological trick that distorted size as well as color.

"I'll be there in a minute. Get everyone out of there—and *hurry!*"

"Okay," Dee said, voice trembling. "I'll do my best—bye . . ."

"No!" Grace shouted into the phone. "Leave the line open, Dee."

"Okay," Dee said quickly, then dropped the phone. Grace could hear the phone clatter against the wall and muffled voices in the background. Then, inexplicably, two voices, a woman's—*Dee!*—and a little girl's—*must be her daughter, Pearl!*—shouting, "Boo!" The clear sounds of gasps and startled cries followed, and then Dee and Pearl were screaming again: "Get out, get out!"

Barreling down the hill toward the traffic light, Grace could hear the scuffling of feet and the screams of the customers as they scrambled in a panic to get out of the diner, dishes crashing to the floor, silverware clattering, and see the effects as people suddenly burst into the parking lot, running for their lives and their cars, looking back over their shoulders in disbelief as a violent argument erupted in the diner.

Dee was suddenly back on the line. "Grace, Grace! Ain't nobody here but ghosts now. Must be forty or fifty of 'em."

"Get out!" There was no need to shout. Grace could hear the phone clattering up against the wall, briefly masking the shouting of the ghosts.

"Where is he?" a man was shouting angrily. *"Where . . . is . . . he?"* Was that Heph? Was he looking for Charlie? And where in hell was Charlie?

Grace had little time to think, or listen. The light at the bottom of the hill had turned red, and a slowly moving caravan of 18-wheelers was rumbling through the intersection. She hit the brakes hard, almost standing on them, the Caddy reluctant to give way to the thrill of momentum.

CHAPTER 42

CHARLIE HAD FALLEN THREE TIMES and was bruised and bleeding when he emerged along the tree line opposite the diner. He couldn't believe his eyes. Customers and staff were running away from the diner, heading for their cars in a panic. Two people were running toward him in the darkness. Jeanie. Chloe.

"Charlie!" Jeanie shouted, rushing up to him, breathless. "Thank god you're not in there!"

"What's going on? Where's Dee?"

"Trapped," Chloe said, pointing back at the diner, "with Pearl and the rest—Jesus, Deuce, Monroe, maybe some customers."

"We barely made it out ourselves," Jeanie said. "Nothin' but ghosts in there now, Dee and Pearl saw to that, made 'em flicker, scared us all to death, let me tell you . . ." Her voice trailed off. Charlie had already turned away and was running for the diner, Chloe giving chase. Jeanie shook her head and ran after them. She knew she'd never catch Charlie, but maybe she could stop Chloe before it was too late.

As Charlie ran, he scanned the diner, looking for Dee and Pearl. He couldn't make out who was fighting, but there was clearly a fight going on. A small group of customers—no, ghosts, my god they're flickering!—were gathered round, while others stayed put on their stools or in their booths, stunned, anxious expressions on their faces as they watched the argument unfold, just as they must have done in life.

As Charlie neared the entrance, Chloe tried to reach out and grab his arm. "No, Charlie, No!" But it was too late; he burst into the diner, all the ghosts turning toward him.

Chloe pulled up short, terrified, and slowly backed away from the diner door, Jeanie coming up behind her and throwing an arm around her shoulders.

"Dear God in heaven," Jeanie said, her eyes, like Chloe's, fixed on Charlie and the ghosts.

CHAPTER 43

GRACE FELT HELPLESS. Every time she thought she had a clear path, another truck would come speeding through, horns blaring, as she inched farther into the intersection. And now, even though the light had changed, cars kept speeding through. She could see the frightened looks of the drivers and passengers. Must be customers.

And then the intersection was clear. She lurched across the road and into the parking lot, spraying gravel as she skidded to a halt next to Chloe and Jeanie. She threw open the door and raced over to them.

"You all right?" she said. "Where's Charlie?"

Chloe was sobbing, unable to speak.

"In there," Jeanie said.

Through the window, Grace could see Charlie, Dee, and Pearl being forced into a corner near the phone, which was still dangling from the wall. *The phone!*

"Dee!" Grace screamed as loudly as she could into her cell phone, hoping her voice would be loud enough for Dee to hear over that dangling phone. It wasn't, but her scream was heard by everyone in the diner, including Dee, who spotted Grace immediately. Grace silently pointed at her cell phone and mouthed, "Phone!"

Dee nodded, slid along the wall, and began reeling it in. When she lifted it to her ear, she only had time to quickly whisper, "They're going to kill us," before Hephaestus ripped the phone from her hands and pulled it from the wall.

"Like *hell* they will," Grace shouted. She *could* not, *would* not, let Charlie come to harm. She'd lost her Bill, but she would *not* lose Charlie. Or Dee. Or Pearl.

She ran headlong for the door, with no more of a plan than to force her way to Charlie. Then something made her pull up short: a man who could not possibly be there, about to enter the diner. *McAllister!*

Grace called out to him. McAllister turned, smiled at her, and then turned back and entered the diner. What happened next made Grace's jaw drop. McAllister entered the diner an old man, but once inside morphed into a younger McAllister, the McAllister who'd owned The Bluebird Diner, the McAllister who'd been at home when the tragedy unfolded in his diner, the McAllister who was here now to set things right. Or make things worse.

Grace wasn't sure what to do next. Call the police? No. Do nothing? After all, McAllister was here to take the blame; surely they wouldn't harm Charlie now.

A glance through the window seemed to prove that theory. Hephaestus was motioning for McAllister to get back against the far wall, the one Davis had built to block the view of the cemetery. He was shouting at him, waving a pistol. "Get back to your window, you fuckin' coward!"

Window? Grace thought. And then it hit her. Of course! She bolted for the Caddy, jumped in, and sped away up the long hill to the college.

CHAPTER 44

Neon Bob was anything but neon-like, with the possible exception of the orange and chartreuse jumpsuit he wore, which glowed in the dark from the black light he'd installed in the cabin of the truck. Other than that, he was a short, bald man as round as a beach ball, with a dour expression fixed on his face, as if lemons made up his entire diet. And he stank—*bad*—of garlic and sweat.

Getting him to talk about anything was like pulling teeth, so Larry tried to keep the conversation, such as it was, focused on Neon Bob's tricked out truck, which featured brightly glowing neon lights, truly a work of neon art on wheels.

Neon Bob had installed neon everywhere. The entire truck was outlined in blue neon, making it look like a ghost truck speeding along toward the Red Oak Diner.

After expressing his awe over the truck, Larry explained in detail the problems with the signs, Neon Bob alternately grunting and shaking his head as Larry described each of the many tests he'd done on the signs.

And Neon Bob was incredulous. "Larry, that's just not remotely possible. The signs just aren't wired that way."

"That may be," countered Larry, "but I know what I saw. Hell, you'll just have to see for yourself."

"This seems like an entire waste of my time, and if it is, you are gonna owe me big time."

And then Neon Bob was standing on his brakes, his truck barely avoiding a collision with a speeding pink Cadillac.

"Holy shit!" screamed Larry.

"What the *fuck!*" said Neon Bob. "Did you see that crazy woman? Man, that was too damn close."

"You got that right," Larry said. "Oh, here we are, turn here."

Neon Bob slowed the truck and turned into the parking lot of the Red Oak Diner. His mouth dropped open.

The shock of the near miss with the Cadillac was nothing compared to what he saw now. Every letter in the diner signs was flashing and flickering, the buzzing sound growing louder and louder until the letters began to explode. Then he noticed two waitresses, screaming their heads off and running toward the woods to escape the flying glass.

"Shit, let's get out of here!" shouted Neon Bob, putting the truck into reverse, then swinging it around, and flooring it, gravel spraying everywhere as the truck hit the highway and sped away.

If Neon Bob had looked in his rear view mirror, he would have seen all the signs go dark. And then he would have seen a few letters in the *DINER* sign flicker and buzz back to life.

D

I

E

CHAPTER 45

CHARLIE FELT LIKE HE WAS WATCHING A PLAY, long practiced, unfold before him. But instead of being in the audience, safely on the other side of the footlights, away from the action, he was onstage, in the middle of things, an actor unsure of his role or his lines.

Once McAllister had come into the diner, the ghosts had turned away from them.

"Places, dammit!" Heff shouted.

The other ghosts scrambled from booth to stool and stool to booth, to position themselves as best they could to match where they had sat or stood that tragic night at The Blue Bird diner.

Some sat in their booths, trying their best to politely ignore the coming heated argument, just as they had done in The Blue Bird. Others looked on, rapt by the unfolding drama. A few seemed to be praying. And one, Deuce, looked like he could barely contain his anger, his fists clenching and unclenching, the muscles of his jaw pulsating, his entire attention focused on Heph.

"And you," Heph shouted at McCallister, "get back to that window!"

Charlie looked over at Jesus and Monroe behind the counter, who were calmly watching the action and whispering to one another.

What's up with that? Charlie thought. He got Monroe's attention and motioned for him to stay put,

Monroe giving him a thumbs up, Jesus looking on, confused. Then Charlie clutched Dee and Pearl to his side and whispered, "Easy, stay close, we'll get out of this."

Dee and Pearl nodded silently, each squeezing him tightly. They were both shaking.

"Whatever happens, stay out of it," he whispered. "Remember, they're already dead." They nodded again.

Charlie told them not to move, at least for now, so they stood there in the corner, watching the argument unfold, distracted only by the sight and sound of Grace speeding away in the Caddy. *Can't blame her for running*, Charlie thought. *She must be scared to death. Who am I kidding? I'm scared to death.* He gave Dee and Pearl a little extra squeeze, and they both looked up at him, their attempts at brave smiles cut short by Heph.

"I *said* get the *fuck* back to your window, you chicken-shit bastard!"

McAllister took one step back, his eyes focused on the gun, but then stopped, a look of resolve on his face. "No, not this time."

"No, Chester!" Martha screamed, running to her husband, putting herself between him and the gun, a shield for the man she loved.

Mindy tried to follow but Heph grabbed her around the waist, tugged her close, and put the gun to her head. "Oh, no you don't."

Martha gasped, then took one step toward Heph, arms outstretched, pleading. "No, no, please don't hurt her!"

Heph grunted derisively. "Move away from him, or I'll kill her. I swear I will."

Martha hesitated.

"Move away!" Heph said through clenched teeth. "I have no fight with you, just this cheatin' husband of yours."

"The deal was *fair*," McAllister said.

"Fair? *Fair?* You and your lawyer cheated me out of thousands!"

"You signed the agreement, so don't go blamin'—"

"Legal *gobbledygook,* and you *know* it." Heph cocked the gun and placed the barrel on Mindy's temple. "Now you're gonna pay."

"No!" Martha screamed. She started to move toward Heph, but McCallister grabbed her and pulled her back.

"Let my little girl go," he said. "Your beef is with me, not them."

"Oh, really?" snorted Heph. "How about this? "First your little girl, then your wife, then you." He looked straight at Martha. "You want your little girl alive, you move away from him."

"Go, dear," Chester said.

Martha looked helplessly back and forth between Mindy and McCallister, frozen to the spot. "Please, don't do this . . ."

"Wait!" someone shouted. It was Deuce, running straight at Heph. "Leave them alone!"

"Deuce, no!" Martha screamed. But it was too late. Heph had raised his gun and fired once into Deuce's chest, throwing him back, his body crumpling to the floor.

Martha instinctively rushed to him, dropping to her knees and cradling his head. "What have you done? He was just a—"

"Kid? Your lover, more like."

"No," Martha said, vigorously shaking her head, tears flowing down her cheeks. "No."

"Ha! I've been watchin' you, lady, and I've seen a thing or two . . ."

"Shut your foul mouth!" McAllister said, taking a step toward Heph, but stopping when Heph leveled the gun at him again.

Heph laughed. "Seems your woman is more interested in the dead than the living. I can fix *that* for you."

He cocked the gun again and put it back against Mindy's head. Martha's eyes grew wide with fright. "No, not Mindy."

"Chester then." Heph said, swinging the gun toward Chester. As Martha scrambled to her feet and raced toward her husband, Heph laughed and began firing.

CHAPTER 46

THE FIRST BULLET CAUGHT MCCALLISTER IN THE NECK, the second in the stomach. He dropped to his knees and fell face down on the floor, Martha, trying to shield him, taking the third bullet in the head.

Four things happened quickly then, distracting Heph, preventing him from firing a fourth bullet, the one he intended for Mindy, who was struggling to break from his grip, her anguished shrieks filling the diner. First, the bodies of Deuce, Chester, and Martha became brilliant balls of light and shot through the roof of the diner.

Then there was Pearl. For her everything seemed to be happening in slow motion. Mindy's mom and dad shot down, crumpling to the floor and then bursting into blinding light. Heph cocking the gun once more and turning it toward Mindy. And the blood, so much blood. Pearl was *not* going to let this happen to Mindy.

She broke free of Charlie's grasp and raced to Mindy.

"No!" Dee screamed, but Pearl was already there.

"Let her go!" Pearl shouted, tugging at Mindy's arm while she kicked Heph repeatedly. Before Dee or Charlie could react, Heph swung his gun, hard, against Pearl's cheek, knocking her to the floor.

And then there was Charlie and Dee, another distraction for Heph as he tightened his grip on Mindy and raised the gun once more to her head. He could see them running toward him. No problem, he'd deal with them first and then take care of the little bitch. He swung the gun around and pointed it at Charlie, but he was too slow. Dee was on him.

"You bastard!" Dee wailed, slamming a fist into his face. She had planned another blow, her left fist curled and ready, but a fourth thing happened, by far the most distracting and startling.

The far wall of the diner, Davis's wall, exploded and Grace's pink Caddy came hurtling into the diner, ghost after ghost flickering and disappearing under its grill, shooting out the back and through the hole in the wall as bright bursts of light, heading heavenward. Charlie and Dee turned away from Heph, who was leveling his gun at Grace, and dragged the still unconscious Pearl out of harm's way. Mindy, too, took advantage of the opportunity, breaking away from Heph and following the others out of the Caddy's path.

Heph was able to get off two shots, the first crashing through the windshield and whizzing past Grace's ear, the second putting a hole in the ceiling as the Caddy hit and ran over him, his body disintegrating, seemingly disappearing into the floor.

The car hurtled onward, barely losing speed, to where Charlie and the others were standing—clearly, not out of harm's way.

CHAPTER 47

THINGS BEGAN TO SLOW DOWN. Grace had the feeling that she had hit a thick, liquid wall, like molasses, the car preternaturally slowing as Monroe and Jesus suddenly appeared in front of the car, brown wings unfolding from their backs, forming a shield to protect the others and stopping the car.

And then it was over, Monroe offering a booming laugh as the Caddy stopped inches from them. "Nice driving, Grace."

Grace sat wide-eyed behind the wheel, her eyes fixed on their wings, which seemed to glow darkly. "Um . . . thanks."

She got out of the car and joined the others, including Chloe and Jeanie, who had rushed into the diner and now stood, stunned and speechless, gawking at the wings on Monroe and Jesus.

Monroe turned to Jesus. "You see? Now *that's* how it's done. Improvisation is *key*."

Jesus shook his head. "But she's the one who—"

"Now, now," Monroe said, "let's not split hairs here. I *gave* her the idea."

"I guess, but—"

"No guesswork involved, sonny boy, and no buts."

"Yeah, well . . ."

"Admit it, Jesus. Why do you think they sent me down to handle this?"

"Well . . ."

"Well? Well?" he said sarcastically. "Is that all you can say?"

Jesus began to speak but stopped when Monroe held a finger to his lips. "Just listen. How many *years* have you been tryin' to set this straight? Showin' up early the way you did, killing all those poor people long before their times?"

He held a finger up again as Jesus attempted to answer.

"Let me answer that—too damn many. And do you have *any* idea what the admin costs alone are for that kind of bungling? Rewriting history is not a laughing matter, my friend. Hell, I read all your simpering reports about that damned wall, and not *once* did you suggest a way to resolve that final detail. Meanwhile, a thousand angels are busting butt reworking *everything*."

"Oh, come on," Jesus said. "Cut me a little slack here. It was my first job—a simple rookie mistake is all—and don't forget there was the matter of the moon."

Monroe laughed. "Moon, *shmoon*, you could have made the moon red, blue, fucking *chartreuse*—any color you wanted, and no one would have been the wiser. No, my friend, it's about innovation, sensing what needs to be done, and doing it."

Jesus shrugged and looked over at Mindy. "What about her—and them?" He pointed at Charlie, Dee, Grace, Chloe, Jeanie, and the now conscious but groggy Pearl, who was staring at them, mumbling, "Momma, are we dead?"

"No, baby, we're alive as can be," Dee said, hugging her close.

"Then *why* are Monroe and Jesus angels . . . and *why* are they *cursing*, momma?"

"I don't know, child."

"A common misconception," Monroe said. "It's not about the words you say, dear, it's about how you live your life."

"Fuckin'-A," Jesus said, winking at Pearl and Dee.

Monroe looked over at Charlie. "Sorry for the mess, boss, but I'll make it right for you. You guys okay?"

Charlie nodded. "I guess, but how . . . I mean who . . ." Actually, he didn't know what the right question was.

"I know," Monroe said, "the wings are pretty startling, huh?"

"But they're *brown*," Pearl said.

Monroe clucked. "Of course they're brown. You're brown, aren't you, and mommy thinks *you're* an angel. Just go with it, girl."

Pearl beamed at him, and Monroe gave her a wink before turning back to Charlie. "That was your question, right, the wings?"

"Well, no," Charlie said. "What I meant was, what just happened here?"

"Oh, *this*," Monroe said, looking around at the wreckage wrought by the Caddy. "Like Jesus said, what we have here is the aftermath of a classic rookie mistake. Heph was supposed to kill McAllister and Deuce and Martha years ago, but that's not the way it went down. Jesus here screwed up and directed the first bullet to the propane tank, thinking it would be the humane thing to do, a quick death and all." He turned to Jesus. "Ain't that right, Jesus?"

Jesus nodded sheepishly and looked down at the floor.

"And the result," Monroe continued, "was McAllister was outside the diner, looking through the window, too cowardly to come in and face Heph. And that's the last image everyone in the diner saw, him cowering there at the window, before they were all blown to smithereens, thanks to Jesus."

"But McAllister said he wasn't there, that he was home sick at the time," Charlie said.

"A lie," Monroe said. "His whole life was a lie after that. He could have rescued them, at least in his own mind, so he had to live with that cowardice every day. Tell yourself a lie long enough and you begin to believe it."

"That's right," Jesus said. "Tell a lie once, it's a lie; tell it twice, and it's a truth by half."

"What?" Charlie said.

"Pay no attention to Jesus," Monroe said. "He just loves to say shit like that."

"But the others," Dee said. "Why were they haunting the diner?"

"A common thing, so common, in fact, that that's my job—making things right. They have a sense, don't ask me how, but they seem to *know* they were taken before their time."

"So they stay." Charlie said.

"Yeah," Monroe said, "they stay until they know things have been set right. Martha knew she was going to die either way, but she couldn't spend all of eternity thinking her husband was a coward."

"And what about those pies?" Dee said. "No one seemed to get enough of those pies."

Mindy, who had been standing quietly until now, too stunned to speak, seemed to awaken with mention of the pies. "My momma, she won prizes for her pies."

Her voice startled everyone, especially Jeanie, who leaned in, cupped a hand over Chloe's ear, and whispered, "How come *she's* still here?"

"Careful," Monroe said, wagging a finger at her. "Angels are all about whispers." And then he turned back to Mindy. "She did indeed," he chuckled. "In fact, that night at The Blue Bird was a special pie night, a celebration of her Blue Ribbon for Best Pie at the county fair."

Mindy beamed. "Some say her pies were charmed."

"Charmed?" Monroe said. "Well, maybe not exactly charmed. The people who died in The Blue Bird? That pie was their last taste of life. That's why they kept clamoring for more."

"That is *so* sad," Chloe said, looking down at Mindy, tears welling in her eyes.

Jeanie threw an arm around Chloe's shoulders and gave her a gentle squeeze. "There, there, dear, they're all in a better place now."

"I still don't get it," Grace said. "The others weren't involved in the dispute, they just happened to be in the wrong place at the wrong time. Why *would* they stay? Not just for pie?"

Monroe sighed heavily. He didn't want to get into all this. "It's complicated. For starters, Heaven and Hell are voluntary; some folks just stick around for a time, sometimes for a long time, sometimes forever."

"Voluntary?" Dee said, "But I thought the good went to Heaven and the bad went to Hell."

Monroe and Jesus exchanged looks, and laughed.

"Not that clear-cut," Jesus said. "Heaven, Hell, they both have open-door policies. You can come and go as you please."

"But why would anyone want to burn in Hell?" Grace said.

Monroe and Jesus exchanged looks again, and laughed.

"Look," Monroe said, "Hell isn't like that, folks. It's more a place where you can raise hell, if you know what I mean, like Vegas or Mardi Gras."

Dee shook her head, incredulous. "But what about the Ten Commandments?"

"Oh, *that*," Jesus snorted. "An early best-seller, I'll give you that and great for crowd control, but the last time I looked nine out of ten was still an *A*, and eight of ten was still a *B*."

"But that would be *sinning*," Dee said.

Monroe and Jesus exchanged looks yet again, shaking their heads.

"That's a term used only on Earth," Monroe said. "Like religion."

"What?" Charlie said. "So you're saying anything goes? Kill someone? Screw your neighbor's wife?"

Monroe raised his eyes to the ceiling, exasperated. "No, killing is bad, for sure. But don't get me started on marriage. That's another purely Earthly convention."

"But—" Charlie began.

"Look," Monroe said, holding up a hand. "I guess to put it simply, God's not looking for perfection, and neither is the Devil. In fact, they're not looking at all."

"What?" Dee and Jeanie said, almost in unison.

"Yeah," Monroe said, "They're pretty much Big Picture dudes—expanding universe, life on other worlds, lotteries, and such."

"But—" Charlie began again, but this time Pearl interrupted him.

"I have a question," she said, raising her hand.

"Sure, kid," Monroe said, tousling her hair.

"In Sunday School, they teach us that evil people will be sent to Hell. You're not saying Heph's going to some place like Las Vegas, are you?"

Monroe chuckled. "No, no, he'll be punished all right." He shook his head and glanced heavenward. "Jeez, it's always this or that with these people down here. Good, evil; life, death; love, hate; drunk, sober; white, black. It's not like that at all. It's way more complicated than you can possibly imagine. Committees are involved. Besides, you wouldn't believe me if I told you. Not now, anyway, while you're living. Best thing is to just wait for your orientation after you die—they'll explain everything then. They've got slide shows and everything."

"But—" Charlie said, but Monroe gave him a stern look.

"No more," he said. "We've got a schedule to keep. So to *your* point, like I said, we don't know why any particular person stays around after death, not really. Oh, there are theories on this particular case. Some angels back at HQ say some of these spirits were held here on Earth by the powerful emotions of Heph and Martha, who needed them as witnesses—actors in the company, extras, if you will—the unintended consequence of ripping the continuum. To set things right, everything had to be played out exactly, every last detail."

"Like the wall," Grace said. "That finally clicked for me, that the window was missing."

"Yes," Monroe said, "the *last* detail."

"So . . . what now?" Dee said. "Is it over?"

"Oh, yes," Monroe said. "Just one more thing to do."

"What's that?" Charlie said.

"Okay, here's how it has to go down. The rules say I can't let you remember any of this, so when Jesus and I leave—and no, he's not *the* Jesus, lord knows—you'll remember nothing and the customers who ran out of here will remember nothing—not me, not him, not nothin' to do with ghosts or Heaven or Hell."

"But what about all this wreckage?" Charlie asked. "The place is a mess."

Monroe looked around. "We'll clean it up, but you have to understand that some events may repeat themselves, like Grace here plowing into the diner again."

"But—"

"But . . . things will be all right. When she comes through that wall again, ain't nobody going to be hurt or nothin'; in fact, you'll think it's kind of funny."

"Funny?" said Charlie. "I don't see how it could be—"

Monroe held up his hand to stop him. "Just you wait and see. Of course, you won't remember *this* conversation, either."

Monroe turned away from Charlie and looked down at Mindy, who was now standing quietly next to Pearl. "You ready? Mom and Dad are waitin' for you."

Mindy smiled at him, nodded, and turned to Pearl. "Thanks for rescuing me. I'm really sorry about that other time."

"No problem," Pearl said, giving her a big smile. "You go see your mom and dad now. Everything's gonna be fine, you'll see. And my guess is you won't have to do math in Heaven."

Mindy giggled, then turned back to Monroe. "I'm ready."

"Hold on tight to my wing, child, and I *do* mean tight. We have a ways to go. Jesus, take care of this mess will you? Man's gotta make a living. Oh, and meet me back at HQ for debrief when you're done."

"Wait!" Pearl shouted. "Does this mean all the ghosts are gone?"

"Oops, thanks for asking," Monroe said. "I almost forgot. Yes there's another one here wants me to give Charlie a message."

Charlie gasped. "Lara?"

"Yes," Monroe said. "She wants you to know that she doesn't blame you for what happened that night."

"But it was *my* fault," Charlie said looking around, hoping to see her, but she did not materialize. "Lara, if I'd only—"

Monroe held his hand up. "No, she's firm about this, Charlie. And one other thing. She likes Dee."

Dee smiled as she moved closer to Charlie and put her arm around his waist. "Thank you, Lara."

"Oh, one last thing," Monroe said. "She says you won't be having those bad dreams anymore."

Charlie was about to say something, but Pearl jumped in front of him. "Are you sure there aren't *other* ghosts here?"

Monroe looked around. Pearl's grandmother, long dead, was standing next to Pearl, looking lovingly down at her. A man in a tri-corner hat, musket in hands, sat on the counter, talking quietly to Charlie's grandfather. Dee's husband was giving Dee dirty looks and trying in vain to remove her arm from around Charlie's waist. Grace's husband, Bill, and the original owner, Davis, were giving Monroe big thumbs up and dancing beside Grace.

Outside, a troop of Civil War soldiers rode by on horses, a stars-and-bars flag whipping in a ghostly wind, as ghosts of every age and era parted to let them through, some waving, some not, all trying as best they could to avoid tripping on the ghostly cats, dogs, and squirrels racing around at their feet.

"Yeah," Monroe said. "They're all gone."

And with one flap of his wings and a blinding flash of light, he and Mindy disappeared through the Caddy hole, his parting laugh filling the diner.

Jesus looked around, sighed, and looked at Grace. "You sure know how to mess up a place, lady. Oh well, to work."

He raised his wings and closed his eyes. And then, just as suddenly, as if he'd forgotten something, he opened his eyes and folded his wings. "Oh, one more thing. All that talk about Heaven and Hell? We were just messin' with you. It's not like that at all."

Everyone smiled, most of all Pearl, who took a step closer to Jesus. "So, there *is* a Heaven and Hell?"

Jesus snorted. "Yeah, sure . . . kinda . . . sorta . . . you'll just have to wait and see. Anyway, back to work."

He raised his wings and closed his eyes, and the whole diner seemed to shudder.

CHAPTER 48

THE SOUND OF THE CADDY HITTING THE DINER'S WALL startled everyone, some customers falling off their stools, some leaping from their booths. Fortunately, the Caddy came to rest halfway inside and halfway outside the diner, looking almost like an intentional, if bizarre, design feature.

Before the dust settled, Charlie and Dee were pulling a stunned but unhurt Grace from the car.

"I'm so sorry," Grace said. "The brakes gave out coming down the hill, and I guess I panicked."

"Don't worry about it," Dee said. "The important thing is you're okay."

"Yeah," Charlie said, shaking his head and smiling. "Besides, I never liked that wall anyway."

"No, really," Grace said, "I'll pay for the damage."

Charlie held up a hand. "We'll work something out." He looked back at the Caddy and laughed. "Maybe we should just keep it the way it is."

Nearby customers began to laugh and applaud.

"Listen," Charlie said, raising his voice so all could hear, "this is Grace Sharp, the former owner of the diner. When I invited her to our grand opening, I never thought she'd do me one better and make a grand opening of her own."

Everyone laughed again, some heartily, some politely, but the laughs that stood out the most were those of Eddie, the diner's angel, and Donnell the cook, each winking at each other as they laughed, perhaps sharing an inside joke known only to them but definitely laughing too hard, Eddie's a high-pitched cackle, Donnell's a booming *har-har-har*, the kind of laughs you'd expect on laugh tracks.

Charlie turned back to Grace. "Welcome to The Red Oak Diner." He swept his arm through the air with a flourish, pointing her toward an empty booth. "How about some coffee and pie? We have *great* pie."

Outside, a once-red moon hung pale in the sky, a curl of dark smoke drifting over it, rising from a campfire deep in the woods.

EPILOGUE

WHEN PAULIE HEARD THE SHOTS, he raced for the diner, pushing limbs and branches aside as he ran headlong through the trees. As he burst into the parking lot, a bright flash of light inside the diner made him pull up short. Years later, when he told his ghost story in Gillie's, the local bar, he would say the diner "rippled," that it was like seeing it through the rising waves of heat from a burning-hot asphalt road. And when the rippling stopped, he told his rapt listeners, there was an eerie moment of stillness, of preternatural silence, before the pink Caddy came hurtling down the hill, crashing into the diner. He warned one and all never to frequent the diner, to keep well clear of it, because ghosts lurked there even now. He knew because he had seen them.

The story raised goose bumps for some, but most just scoffed at the idea, whispering among themselves that Paulie was, after all, a young man who had been in and out of mental institutions the past several years because of his wild, delusional stories about ghosts and missing diner workers, and now was "just a damned fool drunk," as if the truth and liquor were incompatible.

Made in the USA
Middletown, DE
30 June 2025